THE GIRLS ON FLOOR 13

HELEN PHIFER

Storm

Copyright © Helen Phifer, 2024

The moral right of the author has been asserted.

Ebook ISBN: 978-1-80508-521-8
Paperback ISBN: 978-1-80508-615-4

Cover design: Blacksheep
Cover images: Depositphotos, Shutterstock

Published by Storm Publishing.
For further information, visit:
www.stormpublishing.co

ALSO BY HELEN PHIFER

Detective Maria Miller Series

The Haunting on West 10th Street

Her Lost Soul

Annie Graham Series

The Ghost House

The Secrets of the Shadows

The Forgotten Cottage

The Lake House

The Girls in the Woods

The Face Behind the Mask

The Good Sisters

Lake View House

Detective Lucy Harwin Series

Dark House

Dying Breath

Last Light

Beth Adams Series

The Girl in the Grave

The Girls in the Lake

Detective Morgan Brookes Series

One Left Alive

For all the readers who love a spooky story as much as I do, this one is for you. Thank you xx

PROLOGUE

Seventeen-year-old Dory Painter was lying on the bed surrounded by xeroxed photos of the Parker Hotel in New York. To say she was obsessed with the building and its history was an understatement. The red brick, fourteen-story-high hotel was iconic. Once a mecca for all kinds of artists, it had a dark past—and an unusually high number of murders and suicides. The black, wrought-iron balconies—and the fact that it had a floor thirteen—gave it something most other hotels in the city didn't have. Not to mention its history of haunting, which was the real attraction for Dory.

She loved watching reruns of old ghost shows. Her favorite accounts on TikTok showed visits to the haunted Ed and Lorraine Warren Museum. They scared the crap out of her, but she couldn't stop watching. Dory hadn't even heard of the Parker Hotel until she'd stayed there with her parents for a few days, when she realized her favorite TV show had done a three-night special investigating the hotel.

The atmosphere inside its corridors was electric and she'd quickly found herself falling in love. Although they'd stayed on the ninth floor—not the infamous thirteenth—it had still been creepy as hell. Dory had experienced the worst bad dreams of her life on the rollaway cot in that room, dreams of being chased through the empty floors of the hotel by a black shadow. Each morning, she woke up at three am, shivering, her heart racing, relieved that she was sharing a room with her parents and not on her own.

When they went shopping the first day, she begged her mom to leave her at the huge Barnes and Noble on Fifth Avenue for an hour. She found a book detailing the history of the Parker and another which called it "The Most Haunted Hotel in New York". Dory had spent her allowance buying both books, then took them to the coffee shop on the first floor, bought herself an iced coffee and lost herself inside the pages.

Since then, she'd joined a forum for ghost hunters online, looking for anyone who could get her access to the Parker Hotel to do a ghost hunt without getting caught and thrown out.

"Michelle's here."

Her mom's voice broke the trance she was in as she stared at the pictures.

"Tell her to come up."

Michelle's voice drifted up the stairs, as she chatted to Dory's mom. Dory's best friend was the reason her mom left Dory alone much of the time. She trusted her more than she trusted her own daughter. Dory was aware that her attitude wasn't always the best. When she came over, Michelle had longer conversations with her mom than Dory ever did. But that was Michelle. She was one of those people who could talk to anyone about anything. Dory, meanwhile, hated her mom knowing her business. When she tried to talk to her mother about the ghosts at the Parker or the latest episode of *Ghost Hunters*, she just rolled her eyes.

After a soft knock on the door, Michelle stepped inside.

"Your mom is pissed with you for not taking out the trash again—or loading the dishwasher."

"Tell me something I don't know. She's always mad at me about something."

"Why don't you just do it, though? I hate putting out the trash, but if it means my mom won't be nagging me for the rest of my life, I'll do it every day."

"That's cause you're a such a kiss ass. Why don't you go put my mom's trash out while you're at it and save me the hassle?"

Michelle grinned at her, picked up a cushion that had fallen on the floor, and threw it at Dory's head.

"You're a douche, Dory."

"That may be, but I'm a douche with access."

Michelle jumped on the bed next to her. "You found someone?"

Dory nodded. "Found a maintenance guy online who said he could get us into the hotel and up to room 1303."

Michelle squinted at her. "Why would he do that for us?"

"Maybe he's a nice guy who is as interested in the ghosts of the Parker as we are?"

"And maybe he's a creep."

"So what if he is? There are two of us and one of him. We let him give us access to the room, film it, take our shots and whatever else, then thank him and be on our way home before any of our parents realize that we went out of town."

"Yeah, but he might want something in return, Dory."

She shook her head. "Honestly, he seems like an okay guy. He said he hates working on that floor, so much weird stuff happens. He doesn't have a problem with getting us inside as long as we don't take too long. He said he'd accept a coffee as his payment and access to the photos and videos we take."

"No funny business?"

Dory laughed. "What's funny business?"

She made a face. "No sex in return for his favor?"

"Well, it depends—if he's decent looking I might have some fun."

Michelle shuddered. "Don't even joke. In a hotel room where two women were murdered? Yuck, I'd rather not, thank you. That's just weird, Dory."

"Look, we can't afford to rent a room at the Parker ourselves, and there's no guarantee we could get access to *the* room if we did."

"When can we go?"

She grinned. "Tomorrow. I bought the bus tickets already with my left-over Christmas money. You tell your parents you're stopping here; I'll tell mine I'm going to yours. We'll skip school and get the Greyhound to NY. I'm so freaking excited about this, Michelle; we waited months to find someone, and this could be our only chance."

Michelle frowned. "It's all a bit sudden, though. What if the school phone to see why we didn't turn in?"

"We phone the absence line for each other, simple. This is going to be brilliant—we can't not do it. You promised you'd come with me. We could get some amazing footage to show on our YouTube channel when we launch it."

Reluctantly, Michelle nodded. Dory felt bad. She was pushing her friend to do this, but she couldn't let an opportunity like this go. The Parker was calling her to it, and she wasn't about to ignore it.

ONE

The woman in the long, blue dress stared down onto West 23rd Street. She watched the flurry of tiny figures walk by, their heads down, never looking up. Her palms pressed against the thin glass of the window, leaving prints in the condensation. The glass needed replacing, as did the rotting, peeling wooden frames. Every damn thing in this hotel needed ripping out; every fixture and fitting was way past its best. A wave of sadness rushed over her. It was the same every day without fail. The feeling of isolation and desolation was so overpowering she had no choice but to give in to it. She was stuck in a loop, reliving the same day over and over, ever since 1945, always with the same ending.

She had no idea how long this had gone on for, how many days, years, her world had been this way. She watched the people below her going about their business without a second thought for the woman balancing on the precipice of life above them, wishing that just one of them would spare a second to lift their gaze from the sidewalk and see her. It would be so nice for someone to acknowledge her existence, just for once.

Kids were different. Occasionally a hurried parent with a

child dragged behind them would pause, wondering why their kid had suddenly stopped and stared upwards. But even so, kids had no concept of what they were looking at. Now and then, she'd wave, hoping a child below would see her, but they never did. Or if they did, it was brief. She was nothing more than a blue smudge, gone in seconds, as they hurried past, continuing with their lives, as self-obsessed as every other native New Yorker.

She pursed her lips as a sigh escaped them. She felt heaviness pressing down on her shoulders at what she was about to do. She wasn't even sure why she'd done this in the first place. It had been so long ago. Some stupid argument with her daughter, perhaps. They'd often argued over silly little things. All she knew was she was now destined for the rest of eternity to repeat it. A decision had been made, for whatever reason, and there was no going back from it now. It was as if it had been written in the stars, and there was no escape. No escape from this awful hotel. She wished she'd never set foot inside the Parker, but she had, and now she was stuck for the rest of eternity.

She crossed to the queen-sized bed, the one she was supposed to be sharing with her daughter, who was now long gone. She'd gone out one day and decided not to return, and as sad as that made her, she didn't blame her daughter one little bit. Who needed a mother like her? A mother full of such melancholy and sorrow wasn't much fun.

She stared at her withered hand, remembering the accident that had stopped her from pursuing her one true passion in life: sewing and making beautiful clothes. The gown she wore now had been painstakingly sewn by hand, a beautiful silk gown the same color as the bluest sky on a warm, summer day. It was her favorite dress she'd ever created, with every little diamond and pearl sewn on painstakingly by hand. Before her accident ruined everything. It seemed only fitting she should wear this gown for her final journey.

On the bed lay the pair of heavy, brass dressmaking scissors that had once been the tools of her trade and now were nothing more than a dreadful reminder of everything she'd lost. She picked them up, marveling at how heavy they were, how sharp their blades were after all this time, and then without pausing, she used them to cut off her left hand. She severed tendons, muscle and cartilage, blood spurting fast, as the heavy appendage fell onto the white bed linen, staining it a deep crimson.

She felt bad for the maid who was going to have to clean up her mess, for nothing more than the minimum wage. She turned and walked to the window, opening it as wide as she could, and stepped out onto the narrow balcony—then she closed her eyes and threw herself off. As she hurtled down towards the crowd of passing pedestrians, there was no fear; she was finally free and soaring like a bird.

TWO

Homicide detectives Maria Miller and Frankie Conroy from the 6th Precinct were just about to walk out of the door of the office of the Strange Case Review team when the desk phone rang on Maria's side. Frankie shook his head.

"Don't do it. I'm telling you if you do, it's trouble."

Maria, who as always felt a strong sense of responsibility towards her job, stared at the handset willing it to stop ringing. But she couldn't ignore it and reached out to pick it up.

"Miller."

Frankie shook his head and mimed holding a gun to the side of his temple. She turned away. "Uh huh, right. Where at?" She scribbled an address down on a scrap of paper. "I'll go, but I'm not supposed to be on active duty. We're on the weird and wonderful case review team so you're gonna have to find someone from regular homicide to take over from me as soon as they're free."

She hung up and turned to look at Frankie who leaned against the door, next to a faded poster of Mulder and Scully from the X-Files.

"Why did you answer that when I told you not to?"

She shrugged. "Because it's my job and we're still on the clock."

"Jeez, Maria, you really are a pushover. I thought we were going to grab a bite to eat at the Fat Black Pussycat, maybe down a couple of cold beers, before going home to our depressing lives."

"*You* were going to. I never agreed to that. I have a date tonight with Harrison. I was going home for a shower."

"Can't believe you're still stringing the rich guy along. Yet you'd rather go to a double homicide than out for a drink with him. Something's not right there, kid. You need to figure it out."

"Don't call me kid. I have more grey hairs than you do."

Frankie grinned at her. Maria had a band of pure white hair running through her grown-out bangs. She hadn't had more than a few stray grey hairs before she went into the abandoned hospital in Beacon, but the things she'd experienced inside there had scared her so completely it had turned her hair white. Maria was grateful to him for not pushing her to reveal what had happened, other than the official version of the incident that she'd given to everyone.

"I'm not stringing him along. I like him, we have fun. But it's nothing more, okay? And if there's nobody else to go to a double homicide, then I'm going, end of story. I like that we can occasionally keep our fingers in the pie with the normal kinds of cases, and I never said you had to come with me."

He sighed. She knew he would never let her go on her own. He was her best friend, protector and pain in the ass, all rolled into one, and she loved him deeply for that.

The fire trucks were all over the sidewalk and street when they arrived; Maria had to abandon the Honda behind the paramedics. Frankie, meanwhile, was still complaining.

"Why did Tenth Precinct not send someone?"

"Because it was the funeral this afternoon of that officer who got killed last week. They're probably short on staff. Quit complaining, Frankie. I told you I'd manage. You can go home."

He crossed himself. "And there but for the grace of God, you're right. Sorry, I wasn't thinking. It's a sad day for those guys. I guess we'll cut them some slack."

Crowds of people milled around outside on the sidewalk, huddled in groups. Maria stared up at the Parker Hotel. For a split second, she was sure she saw a woman in blue staring out of the upper floor window, looking down at her. Maria tugged on the arm of the firefighter standing beside her.

"Hey. Has the building been completely evacuated? There's someone looking out of that window."

He cupped his hand across his forehead and stared up. "Should have been, but it's a hotel, there's a lot of people around and it's pretty hard to make sure they're all out. Besides, the fire was contained on the thirteenth floor. Some quick-thinking guest saw smoke billowing out from underneath the door and hit the alarms. Then she ran to get the extinguisher off the wall and managed to keep it under control. Saved a hell of a lot of lives and the building. Only the room it was started in is smoke-damaged. It didn't have the chance to get going."

Maria nodded. "Brave guy."

The firefighter pointed to the back of the open ambulance where a woman with honey-colored, soot-stained hair and dark smudges across her cheek sat with a foil blanket around her shoulders.

"Brave gal. She's over there."

Maria nodded. It was wrong of her to assume he was talking about a guy, when she knew fine well that she'd go into a burning building to save someone without a care for her own safety. Hadn't she gone into a haunted hospital to find a missing girl and bring her home safely, even when the odds were stacked way against her?

Without realizing she was doing it her fingers reached up and gently touched the streak of white hair she'd come out of Beacon Hill with. Before going into that hospital on her own, she'd had a full head of thick, black, wavy hair with only a few strands of grey running through it. Now, as Frankie liked to remind her, she looked more like Lily Munster than Lily did.

Maria headed towards the woman in the ambulance and held out her hand. "Detective Miller. You did a great job. Fast thinking probably saved an awful lot of lives and the hotel a lot of money."

The woman, who Maria placed in her forties, took her hand and shook it. "My name is Mina Barrow. Thanks, but not so great for whoever was inside that room. I was too late to help them."

"Hey, you did good. They were most likely already deceased long before you knew about the fire. That's out of your control."

"I know, but I still wasn't expecting to see them like that."

Frankie joined them, and asked, "Like what?"

Mina shuddered. "On the beds, just staring into space. And with no feet. Just bloodied stumps. They look like they're just kids, too. God rest their souls."

"Kids?"

"Teenagers, maybe fifteen or sixteen. Far too young to be in a hotel like this in downtown New York."

"Are you staying here, Mina?"

Mina nodded. "I'm in a long-term rental unit on the tenth floor. I couldn't afford the rent on my uptown apartment when I got let go. Split up with my partner and decided I'd rather move downtown and try to manage on my own than stay with that piece of work."

Maria gave her a sympathetic nod. "What were you doing on the thirteenth floor if you live on the tenth?"

Mina's eyes narrowed. "What, am I a suspect?"

"Of course not, unless you give me a good reason to make you one. I'm curious to know why you'd stop off at the thirteenth."

Mina released an epic sigh. "I always use the stairs. Can't afford a fancy gym membership. If I hadn't been heading up to the roof for a quick smoke before going out to the library, I wouldn't have seen it, and this shithole would be a smoldering wreck. I could smell the smoke in the stairwell when I got to the thirteenth floor and thought I'd better go check it out. I don't particularly love the place, but it's home and it's better than a shop doorway if you get my drift."

Maria felt a pang of sadness for the soot-stained woman staring back at her. She'd probably had it all and lost it, yet she still carried on, when she could have hit rock bottom.

"How did you know about the bodies?" Frankie asked.

"The door wasn't locked. I kicked it open with the fire extinguisher and sprayed foam everywhere. I could see them lying there on those twin beds, not moving, and I shouted at them, thinking maybe they were stoned or drunk. I pulled my scarf across my face and ran towards the first bed; the girl was stone cold. My prints are probably on her arm. I tried to shake her awake, but I saw the bloodied stumps where her feet should be and realized she was cold and stiff."

Maria nodded. "Then what?"

"I got the hell out, raised the alarm and rang the fire department. Now here I am talking to you guys."

"Yeah, sorry about that. I expect you want to get back inside and shower. Do you have any injuries that need looking at?"

Maria knew the woman would say no even if she did. Medical bills were expensive, and the insurance was just as bad. Mina shook her head. "Apart from the shock of seeing those girls like that, I'm okay."

"Well, thank you, but if you do have any injuries, they can

be taken care of. If the cops send you to the ER, it doesn't cost you. We appreciate everything you did, Mina."

Mina shrugged. "I'm good, but thanks. I didn't know that."

Maria and Frankie began to walk away, but Maria paused, turning back. "Did you see anyone loitering in the hallways? Did you recognize the girls? Ever seen them in the hotel before?"

"Nope to all of those questions. Sorry, I've told you what I know. There are always people loitering in the hallways. It's that kind of place. But not today. Today it was eerily quiet, considering there was smoke billowing out from underneath that door."

Maria looked up to count the floors, and realized it was the tenth floor where she'd seen the person in blue at the window. She turned back to Mina.

"I saw someone looking out of the window on the tenth floor. She was wearing a blue dress."

Mina shrugged. "And?"

"I wondered if you knew any of the other tenants up there."

Mina shook her head. "You know what, I thought I saw someone in a blue dress standing in the corridor, but it was smoky, and it was only for a second, and then they were gone. This place is crazy. I don't want to know any of my neighbors, if you get my drift. Bad enough I'm living here. I don't need no charity cases on my doorstep. You should ask Rickie, the manager. He knows everyone, although I don't think he keeps an eye on what they're wearing."

"When you say they were gone, gone where?"

"Disappeared into thin air. I probably imagined it, or it was wisps of smoke."

Maria smiled. Why was she so bothered about the person in the window? The fire was out; they were in no danger. But something about the way they'd been staring down had unsettled Maria. It was also strange that Mina had seen a flash of blue outside the room where the bodies had been found. Maria knew what the urban legends said about this hotel: that it was haunted. The most haunted hotel in New York City. But she was here to deal with the murders. The case didn't fit the criteria for the Strange Case Review team to investigate. They walked towards the rear of the car. It was time to get suited up, then go take a look at the scene for themselves.

THREE

By the time they were dressed in protective suits, boots and gloves, the fire chief gave them the go-ahead to enter the building. The duty manager, who Maria assumed was Rickie, was having an animated phone call. Whoever he spoke to must have been stressed judging by the amount of swearing echoing through the speaker.

Frankie headed towards the elevator and Maria caught his arm, pointing towards the stairs. There were fire officers with hoses everywhere.

He shook his head. "The fire is out. There's no danger now."

She supposed he had a point. Nobody stopped them when Frankie pressed the call button, so she assumed they were good to continue. They travelled to the thirteenth floor in silence. The creaking, clanking elevator made them hold their breath, fearing they'd get stuck between floors. With a sudden jerk, it juddered to a halt, before the rattling doors slid open.

Maria led the way. As always, it made her feel better if she could see the body or bodies first, instead of hiding behind Frankie's broad shoulders. There were a couple of fire officers in the hallway—which was desperately in need of decorating. The old-fashioned wallpaper was dark and gaudy with some awful abstract pattern that hurt her eyes. Strips peeled away from the corners of the walls. Maria couldn't think of a worse place to find yourself booked into for a city break. It gave off serious depressing vibes, not the sort of hotel you'd recommend to your friends unless you hated them.

"Are we good to take a look?"

One of the fire officers nodded. "All yours. Our investigators are on the way. When they get here, you can battle it out between you about who's running the show."

Maria smiled at him. Underneath the yellow helmet and streaks of dirt and grime on his cheeks, his eyes were the most beautiful green she'd ever seen, with tiny flecks of gold running through them. She wondered if he was wearing contacts, although if they were they must be expensive.

The door to room 1303 was wide open. Water puddled on the carpet, making it sodden and spongy to walk on. Maria was glad she wore sneakers and not pumps. Frankie, on the other hand, had his expensive Italian brogues on, and she knew he was going to complain for the next hour about ruining his shoes. Despite the fact she told him regularly to save those shoes for best, he didn't listen. When working, he liked to wear a snappy suit, shirt and tie along with his fancy shoes, even though they weren't at all practical.

Maria stepped over the pools of water into the room. On twin beds were the bodies of two fully clothed, teenage girls. The sight of their bloodied stumps where their feet should have been made Maria's stomach clench tight. She hoped to God that whoever did this had removed their feet once they were dead, not while they were still able to feel it.

"Why? Why the hell would you want to remove their feet? What the hell is he going to do with them?" Despite the horror, she struggled to tear her gaze away. Both bodies had deep, thin grooves around the girls' necks; whoever had done this must have been strong.

"Garroted," whispered Frankie behind her. "Had to have used something to do it fast, so he could kill them both before they managed to escape. Manual strangulation can take a long time. Otherwise, while he attacked the first one, the other could have made their escape."

"Not if they were restrained."

"Why didn't they scream? Surely somebody would have heard them."

A loud voice behind them made them both start, and they jumped back from the body.

"Good afternoon, Maria, Frankie. Do you want to let me take a closer look? I might be able to tell you what's happened here." Doctor Betsy Conner was smiling at the pair of them.

Frankie grinned back. "Well, if it isn't my favorite medical examiner. How you doing, doc. You're looking good if you don't mind me saying."

"All the better for seeing you guys. Though I thought you weren't working active cases? I was gutted when I got told you were moved to something else, something top secret."

Maria gave the woman a warm smile. She was one of the good guys. She always made working a homicide that much easier with her willingness to cooperate and keep them up to date with findings.

"Technically we're not, but Maria answered the phone on the way out of the office." Frankie did an exaggerated eye roll of epic proportions. Maria crossed her arms and glared at him.

Betsy smiled. "Well, I'm glad you're here now. May I?"

Frankie did a little bow as he stepped out of the way and winked at her.

They both stepped away from the beds to give her space to work. She took one look at the missing feet and sighed. "What the hell do you suppose he's going to be doing with those?"

"I'm not sure I want to know," muttered Maria.

Betsy nodded, picking up the hand of the girl on the bed nearest to her. "No defensive wounds. This one didn't put up a fight." She walked to the other and stared at the palms of the hands of the second girl, which were facing upwards. "Neither of them did. I'll take fingernail scrapings and clippings from victim one before I touch victim two." She turned back to examine the first girl's wrists. "No marks, so they weren't tied up or restrained. I suppose the tox results are going to come back as positive for drugs and/or maybe alcohol. There is no way you would watch some creep strangle then cut off your friend's feet and not try to escape, unless you were unable to."

"My thoughts exactly." Was he trying to flirt with her? Jeez, she hoped not. There wasn't a more inappropriate place to come on to someone than a murder scene. Or was he just being his usual brazen self? Maria had a sneaking suspicion that now he was a free man he was putting himself out there. She wanted to tell him to pack it in. Instead, she tugged his arm and he looked at her. When she raised an eyebrow, he shrugged.

"Will you be attending the autopsy? It won't be tonight. I might be able to squeeze them in tomorrow after lunch if you're free?"

Maria opened her mouth to say probably not, but he beat her to it. "Sure thing, doc, be like old times, eh? It's been too long. Be good to catch up with you. Maybe we could go for a drink and grab a bite to eat?"

Maria ignored Frankie and smiled at Betsy. "We'll leave you to it. If it's not us, I'll give you a ring and let you know who's taking over. Good night."

Maria took hold of Frankie's elbow and pushed him out of the hotel room into the corridor where the fire officer with green eyes was slowly folding up the hose. He smiled at her and she nodded, then turned to Frankie and hissed, "What was that?"

"What?"

Aware there were too many ears listening in, she walked away, leaving him shrugging at the fire guys. She knew without even turning around that he would be mouthing the word 'women' while holding out his hands as if he was clueless. She made her way to the elevator and waited for him to join her. When they were both inside, he looked her in the eye.

"Wanna tell me what that was about?"

"You blatantly hitting on the doc at a murder scene, like a dog on heat. What's wrong with you, Frankie? That was shameful. You're not that desperate for a date. If you are, get yourself down to the Fat Black Pussycat and pick up a broad there. Don't be doing it on my watch. I don't like it."

He had the decency to look down at his feet. She didn't know what was going on with him. As the elevator doors opened, she saw Rickie ushering guests back inside. He greeted them all by name, which impressed her. Maria couldn't remember what was on her grocery list most days, never mind the names of hundreds of people. She knew she should let it go, but found her feet striding in his direction anyway. He smiled at her, and she couldn't help but smile back.

"This isn't relevant to the fire or the murders—at least, I don't think it is—but do you know the resident on the tenth floor who didn't leave the building? I saw her staring down at the street when we arrived and wondered if they were okay. They might need checking in on or at least updating as to what's happened."

His tanned face seemed to lose its healthy glow. "This person, were they dressed in blue?"

He carried on greeting people as they filed back inside.

"Yes."

"That guest never leaves. They've been here a very long time."

"You know them? They're okay then?"

He shrugged. "I couldn't say whether she's okay or not

because I've never spoken to her personally. But I can tell you
for certain that the woman in blue never leaves, because she's
been dead for eighty years."

A large man, with a chihuahua tucked under his arm and a
straw hat, curled one finger at Rickie, who excused himself and
rushed over to him.

Maria felt a wave of déjà vu rush over her. She felt sadness
mixed with longing, then the sensation was gone, leaving her a
little woozy. For some reason, she was relieved that Frankie was
already outside and hadn't heard this piece of information.

She looked around the tired reception area that had been
considered grand back in its heyday. The glass chandeliers
needed dusting, the marble and gold floor tiles looked as if they
could do with a good sweep and mop. The brass fittings hadn't
been polished until they sparkled for at least forty years,
judging by the dullness they exuded. If Maria closed her eyes,
she could almost imagine the hotel as it was, a bustling hive of
activity, tourists, and guests full of excitement and wonder, their
adventure in the Big Apple about to begin.

A soft vibration under her feet made her open her eyes as
she swayed a little, in the way she did after a couple of cocktails
with Harrison. Somehow, she knew this place; she could picture
it, but not as it was now, as it used to be. That thought disturbed
her a lot more than she'd like to admit.

Snapping herself back to the present, she turned and
pushed her way through the steady line of people filing back
inside, relieved to be back in the New York City air.

FOUR
MAY 1970

New York City reminded him of a broken, sleazy whore.

The unexpected spring heatwave was unbearable as he tried to navigate the streets without getting lost. One wrong turn and he could end up heading for the Bronx or Harlem and he knew he wouldn't survive long in either of those neighborhoods. They'd eat an overweight, white guy for breakfast and spit him out, along with the four wheels of his rusted Cadillac. Women he could control—strapping men he could not.

He searched for the Parker Hotel. He'd heard from a friend of a friend it was the kind of place you went to if you didn't want anyone knowing your business, and he had some business to take care of. The first time he'd visited, he'd left the hotel staff with quite the gift. Those two whores had been so tanked up on grass and cheap bourbon they hadn't even put up a fight. That was a month ago and now it was time to return. Enough time had passed that they wouldn't remember him—he hoped. After all, he was using a different name, a different suit. He didn't need anyone sticking their oar in. He only had thirty-six hours to find what he was looking for and take care of the pressing need that was getting harder to ignore with every hour that passed.

Saint Mary was at home with the two brats, who he'd never wanted but had been lumbered with anyway. She'd been about to enter the convent when they met. She was a shy woman, and a little on the chubby side, like him. He could tell right away she'd do anything for a bit of flattery, even from a creep like him. He'd gone in for the kill after bumping into her outside the diner on the corner of Emerson in Berkeley Heights, his home-town, and she'd fallen for him, in more ways than one. It had been fun in the beginning. She was a virgin, and he'd been having sex with cheap sluts and prostitutes since he began working it. Within two weeks she'd moved into his basement apartment, and within three months she was pregnant.

In the beginning, she couldn't get enough of him. It had been good while that lasted. But he soon got fed up with her taking up space in his apartment. He could no longer do what-ever he wanted. She was most upset when he told her he wanted to whack off to a porno of some strangled whores, and had kneeled on the floor praying to God to forgive him of his sins. So he tried to make her leave, but she had nowhere to go. She couldn't go to the convent now, not in her condition, and she couldn't go home either. She was from a strict, religious family who'd disown her if they found out she'd been screwing the pants off him several times a day when she should have been serving Jesus.

That was six years ago. They'd moved to a bigger apartment when his ability to sell encyclopedias to anyone brought in more money than he ever realized it could—alongside the money he made from forging checks from the old-timer guys and gals who let him into their homes. They'd leave him sitting on the couch, checkbooks nearby, while they got him a drink. By the time they came back, he'd have taken the last check out of the book. Then he'd watch them sign for the brand-new set of encyclopedias they just couldn't live without, for the grandkids who would get so much use out of them. Then he'd thank them for their time, pocket the check, copy the signature while sitting outside their duplex or condo, drive to the nearest bank and deposit it, just like that. Easy as taking candy from a baby. He'd been doing that for over two years now; it was his little bonus for being a good salesman.

He turned onto 23rd Street and recognized the rows of metal balconies that signaled the Parker. He was so charged with electricity that he felt as if he could zap the first person he came across with his finger and watch them jolt out of their skin. He knew where to find the girls he was looking for: the bus station was full of runaways and hopeful teenagers getting off a bus straight out of Hicksville and into the bright lights of the city. If that didn't turn up the kind of girls he was looking for, there was always Times Square, which was full of hookers. But then he'd have to get a cab back to the hotel, and that meant a witness. At least he had the brains to book a room under a false name, and as far as Mary knew, he was at a conference in New Jersey. First, he had to find somewhere to park his car where the wheels would still be attached when he returned. The city was rough, the streets were mean, but none as mean as he was.

He glanced down at the black, patent leather stiletto on the passenger seat next to him. Reaching out, his fingers trailed along the shiny, cool material into the soft lining. He had to squeeze his legs tight to stop himself from getting too excited. Wilma had been a willing participant in his games until it got a little rough and she'd tried to fight back, realizing the money wasn't worth the pain. The more she'd fought, the more excited he'd got. When it was over, he'd cradled her cold, lifeless feet in his hands, sobbing with pleasure and guilt at what he'd done. The guilt didn't last long. Not when he clocked the two smooth, almost perfect feet that were now his to keep and do with what he wished.

He'd managed to remove the left foot, but it had made a real mess. He'd panicked, worrying the motel night clerk would recognize him. Stupid mistake. He should have gone somewhere he'd never stayed before. He bundled the foot up into the yellowed pages of a *New York Times* he found in the bottom drawer and placed it into one of Mary's large plastic Tupperware containers. Then he'd tucked the box into a grocery sack along with both of her shoes. He could take it home and paint the toenails whatever color he wanted. Mary refused to paint her fingers and toes, which was just as well because it might send him over the edge. At least this way he could keep Wilma's shoes with him in the car, as a little reminder of the kind of fun he could have if he really wanted.

FIVE

Outside, as they stripped off the protective suits, Addison, their lieutenant, who was in charge of homicide, pulled up with Cooper. They strolled towards them. Addison had a tendency to send a shower of spittle in whoever's direction he was talking to. He nodded at them in greeting.

"What's the story? Why are you guys here?"

Maria took a step backwards, not wanting him to get too close. Frankie answered before she could, pointing his thumb in her direction. "Miller decided it was her civic duty to attend. I'm just here for moral support."

Cooper shook his head. "Well, you can go home now. I have this covered."

Maria stared at him to see if he was being serious, realizing he was. "Actually, I think there could be something that fits with the criteria for our department, so it makes sense we carry on." She had no intention of telling him she thought she might have seen a ghost. She also had no idea if it was connected to the dead girls, but something told her not to walk away, and she trusted her instinct.

Cooper rolled his eyes and waved his fingers in the air.

"Woowoo, woowoo, it's the twilight zone. Is there a room full of ghosts? Don't tell me. The killer is an escaped demon."

Maria tried to think of a calm, respectable reply, then opted for, "Screw you, Cooper, you're an asshole."

Frankie sniggered and Addison held up his hands. "Kids, behave. Cooper, watch your mouth—you know they're running a legitimate department. Miller, walk me through what you have." He took hold of her elbow and led her away from Frankie and Cooper. Stepping over the fire hoses and puddles of water pooled on the sidewalk, they stopped a safe distance out of Cooper's hearing.

"You're right, he *is* an asshole. But he's the only one I've got free to work this, so tell me why you think I should let him off the hook and give it to you."

"There's something going on with this place. I saw a figure watching the street when we arrived, and the duty manager said it was the resident ghost."

Addison shrugged. "I need more than that. Half of the buildings in the city have tales of ghosts that haunt them."

"I have a feeling that there's a lot more to this than we can see. It's hard to explain. Look, I don't want a double homicide investigation, but something is telling me not to walk away. But if you want Cooper to work it, then it's fine. Come back to me when he's going around in circles."

"You have a feeling?"

She didn't look away from him, despite feeling heat rise into her cheeks. She nodded. He looked at her, then up at the building, before turning back to stare at Cooper.

"Frankie, is he going to be happy to work this?"

She shrugged. "We're a team. He will do what he has to."

"Take me up to the room and talk me through it. I'll tell Cooper he's off the hook."

"Thank you, sir."

"I don't know why you're thanking me; Frankie is going to be pissed. I can tell by the way he's watching our conversation."

"He'll be fine. He's just hungry."

She watched as Addison broke the good news to Cooper, who looked even angrier than Frankie did, but he turned and headed back to the car. Addison suited up then pointed to the hotel entrance. "Show me what you have, Miller."

"Yes, sir. There are two bodies, both females, look to be around late teens. The M.E. is up with them. They're both missing their feet."

Addison stopped dead in the middle of the sidewalk. "They're what?"

"He took their feet, cut them clean off. I have no idea why. At least, not yet."

He scrubbed a hand across his clean-shaven chin, a habit of his when he was stressed or perplexed. They squeezed through the throng of people congregating in the hotel foyer and Maria noticed Addison peering around at the tired decor.

"This place was so grand, so beautiful back in its prime. It's sad to see it looking so rundown. I suppose at least it's still open. Stanley, the manager back in the day, was a great guy. I did my beat shifts around this area and spent a lot of time here. Shooting the shit and drinking coffee with Stan. He was a funny guy. He knew everyone by name, knew their likes, dislikes. How he kept the place running so smoothly was a testimony to his management skills. It broke his heart when they had to shut it down back in the early aughts. Said it was the hotel's way of saying goodbye to him, that it couldn't carry on without him."

"That's sad. What happened to him?"

Addison shrugged. "Retired, down in Brooklyn. Said he'd always wanted to go to Florida but when it came down to it, he couldn't leave New York. Brooklyn was the furthest he could go. He could still see the skyline when he got homesick for this place."

"Wow, that's dedication."

In the lift, Maria pressed the button for the thirteenth floor.

"I'm not sure if it's dedication or madness. He spent his whole life here. I think the building got a hold of him, making him reluctant to leave. I don't even know if he's still alive. He must be in his nineties now, God bless him."

Maria looked around and wondered how it was possible to become so attached to a building.

Addison continued, "Of course, this isn't the first murder to have happened here. At one point it was murder central. But that's going back decades. The sixties and seventies were a wild time for murder sprees."

She looked at him, trying to guess his age. She didn't think he was old enough to have worked in the seventies. "How do you know? You're not that old."

The elevator doors pinged open, and he laughed. "My pa worked this beat before I did. He was friends with Stan, too. He used to tell me all sorts of things about this neighborhood, but it was the Parker where everything happened. I haven't thought about this place in a long time. I've forgotten most of what went on. I just know it had an awful lot of tragedy for a tourist spot."

"Did you hear about the woman in blue on the tenth?"

He shrugged. "I vaguely remember something about that. She checked in and never checked out. But Maria, I think every single hotel in the city can boast about that one. How many guests have died of natural causes, not to mention the suicides in the hundreds of hotels around here?"

Maria pointed to the open door of room 1303 where the crime scene techs were busy setting up and Betsy was packing samples into her case. She smiled at them both.

"Lieutenant."

He nodded. "Hey, doc."

"I'm done. Happy for you to move the bodies when you've finished processing the scene."

"Thanks, I'll be in touch. Maria, are you the lead detective?"

Addison smiled. "She is now."

Betsy arched an eyebrow, not saying a word. She didn't need to; Maria knew what she was thinking. That she'd been pushed to run this case. Maria would let her know at the autopsy that she'd been the one to request it.

Maria, who had removed her crime scene suit at the car, waited in the corridor for Addison to take a look at the bodies. When he came out, his eyes were shinier than they had been. It got to them all. Different cases, different circumstances. He had a daughter not much older than the two girls who'd been murdered, their bodies desecrated so brutally. In fact, it had been his daughter Gina who'd been instrumental in digging up long-forgotten articles on the murder from the 1950s at the house on West 10th St.

"We need to find this asshole, Maria. Christ knows what he's going to do with their feet, but I don't like it, not one little bit."

She nodded. "The hotel must have camera footage. There are cameras all over the place. If they didn't pick him up coming in, then surely the lift or the hallway camera would have got him. I'm going to speak to the manager, Rickie, and request that he go through them now. There are also the cameras out on the street. We should be able to pick them up coming into the hotel and who they're with. We need to identify them fast. Doc, did you find anything?"

She shook her head. "I'll do a thorough search at the mortuary."

"Maria, we found two purses stuffed in the bottom drawer." Tiffany, one of the crime scene techs, hollered from inside the room, and Maria felt a tiny spark of hope that this was going to be the first of many leads to come their way. Tiffany appeared at the doorway holding out two driving licenses.

"Damn, they're both kids, only sixteen and seventeen. Dory Painter and Michelle Carter."

The wave of sadness that washed over Maria almost knocked her off her feet, and she had to reach out a hand against the wall to steady herself. Teenagers, probably on their first big adventure without their parents, or possibly runaways.

"Where are they from, Tiff?"

She looked down at the two pieces of plastic, one in each gloved hand. "Boston."

Maria sighed. How did they get here? She couldn't see them flying into the city, but she wouldn't rule it out. Her best guess would be either train or bus. "When you check their purses, can you see if there are travel tickets? I need to know how they got here so we can go check the CCTV."

Tiff nodded. "Sure thing, Maria, will let you know ASAP."

"Thanks, Tiff, you're the best."

The short Black woman, who had pink and purple dreads hidden under the hood of the white Tyvek suit, laughed. "Flattery is good."

Maria winked at her. "No flattery, I mean it. Thank you."

Addison had regained some of his composure. He walked back towards the elevator. "I'll leave it with you then, Maria."

She watched him go. He'd been subdued, which was good. It meant he hadn't bathed her in spittle. She felt a little bad for him. He was a good boss even if he was a grouch at times. She hadn't realized this until he had put her and Frankie on the West 10th St case.

Waiting until the doors closed, she followed him. This time she pressed the button for the tenth floor. For her, that number would forever be associated with haunted houses.

As the doors opened, she felt a draft of freezing air rush at her face, chilling her body to the bone. This hallway was darker than the thirteenth floor above. She wasn't sure why she was up there; she wouldn't be able to explain it if she was asked. She'd felt drawn to it. Looking down the long corridor, she had no idea which was the room she'd seen the smudge of blue staring down at her from. She should have asked the hotel manager, Rickie.

Slowly, she walked down the hallway, focusing on the rooms facing the street. There was a faint odor of something sour lingering in the air. Her fingers trailed along the wall, touching each heavy wooden door in turn. She didn't feel anything in particular until she reached the last one, when a jolt in her fingertips made her withdraw her hand. Her fingers felt numb with cold. She pressed the palm of her hand against the door to see if she was overreacting, but her skin was suddenly painfully cold and once more she pulled it back sharply.

It reminded her of the attic door in Beacon Hill Asylum. That had been one terrifying attic and she didn't want to repeat that experience. But this was only a hotel room, it didn't lead anywhere except for this floor. How bad could it be? Leaning on the door, she whispered, "I saw you looking, can I help you?" There was nothing in return but silence. Maria stepped away. She was ready to get out of there.

She went to leave to find Frankie, when a low, deep voice whispered, "I saw you looking." It was so close to her ear that she felt cold breath against her neck. The voice didn't belong to a woman. It was deep, gruff almost. Maria jumped and turned so fast that she made herself dizzy. There was no one there— and yet she couldn't shake the feeling that someone was watching her. She regretted coming up here alone. Not wasting any more time, she hurried towards the elevator, jabbed her finger on the call button and prayed that it wouldn't take forever. She didn't look back.

SIX

Frankie chatted to the fire crew who'd almost finished packing their equipment away. He noticed her walking towards him and frowned. Meeting her at the Honda, he climbed inside, and she decided not to tell him about the voice. After all, she could have been imagining it. Given the last couple of months, she was bound to be a bit on edge—it was only natural. Nobody could experience the things she had and not be edgy. The demon on West 10th St, the soul collector at Beacon Hill, not to mention her trip through time that took her back to the sixties to rescue Riley Holt, leaving her with a white streak running through her bangs.

Maria glanced up to the tenth floor, not sure what she was expecting to see. She saw nothing—no flash of blue, nothing dark and scary. Just a row of windows with black cast-iron balconies that were no longer accessible from the rooms as the windows had been fastened shut and air con installed years ago.

"So, are you going to tell me what's wrong with you?"

"Nothing. It's just the shock of those girls. Tiff found their licenses; they are sixteen and seventeen from Boston. Frankie, why the hell has the perp taken their feet? What purpose has he got with them?"

"Do you need me to spell that out for you?" He glanced at her, and she wanted to say no, he didn't have to. "He must have a foot fetish, because you know I can't think of any other reason why he would do that to them. Bad enough that he's strangled them to death, but to pose them and then cut off their feet..."

Frankie's whole body shuddered. "Jerry Brudos."

"Don't know him."

"Good, I'm glad. He was a serial killer back in sixty-eight, sixty-nine. He was a real creep—he had a shoe fetish that started when he was a kid. I remember reading about him years ago. He cut off one victim's foot and kept it in his freezer."

"I know the case you're talking about, just wasn't familiar with his name—he was a real piece of work. You think this guy's a copycat?"

"Possibly. Whatever he is, I don't see this being his first venture into the criminal lifestyle. To murder two teenage girls in a hotel room, cut off their feet and set the room on fire kind of speaks volumes to me. I think he has a varied criminal history. He may not have killed before, but I bet there's a list of charges against his name for lewd behavior."

"Fire officer thinks he started the fire to burn the evidence. Only, lucky for us, he did a poor job of it. Mainly smoke damage."

Maria nodded. "We need to go back and speak to the manager." She slammed the palm of her hand against her forehead. "We haven't door knocked, got a list of guests or found out who paid for the room." She got out of the car and waited for him to turn the engine off and join her.

He shrugged on the sports jacket he'd thrown into the back of the car. "To be fair, we didn't do that stuff because we were only first responders. We weren't expecting to work the case, were we?"

She felt guilty. They should have been home. They'd already worked a long, boring day shift. The unit had been relatively quiet with no major cases since Beacon Hill, only a couple of reports of residual hauntings that weren't linked to any crimes—that had been it. Which was nice, because it proved that not all ghosts were bad. Now, she was making Frankie hang around for the next couple of hours.

"Before we go back inside, tell me Addison agreed the overtime."

That was another thing. She hadn't actually asked him if he would approve overtime pay; she'd assumed it was okay.

"Maria, if you have me busting my ass for the rest of the evening for no pay, I'm not speaking to you for the next week. Cooper is probably on lates. He could be doing all this legwork while we eat burgers."

"Sorry. I'll check with Addison now that it's paid overtime."

He shook his head but headed back towards the black-and-white canopy where huge, glass doors would take them back inside the foyer. Maria sent a quick message to Addison, and hoped he'd read it before he went home. A hungry Frankie was hard work. An underpaid and hungry Frankie was damn near impossible to manage. She needed to remember this before taking on huge tasks that could take hours.

Catching up, she rushed inside to see Rickie standing behind the desk. They say a face can paint a thousand pictures and right now Maria reckoned he was wearing at least five different expressions.

She waved at him and yelled, "Hey, can we talk with you?" She wanted to catch him before he scuttled off somewhere and couldn't be found. He nodded, shoulders sagging, and Maria thought that he wanted to be anywhere but here—but then when did anyone want to be here?

Frankie leaned across the dull, cherrywood reception desk, his arms folded, and smiled. "Hey, Rick—do you mind if I call you that or do you prefer Rickie? 'Cause I like Rick; it's sharper, snappier, hipper."

"You can call me what you want, sir."

Frankie nodded. "That's good. We're getting off to a great start, Rick. Now, my partner and I are going to be hunting down the son of a bitch who killed those girls up on thirteen, and the best way for us to do that is to have your full, undivided attention. Have we got that, Rick? Are you ready to give us everything we need and ask for?"

His head moved up and down fast and his lips peeled back into a smile, revealing his uneven teeth. "What do you need?"

Maria took over. Now that Frankie had done his bad cop routine, she would be good.

"We need a copy of the guest register, either printed off or emailed directly to us; a list of anyone who stays here who you think, in your professional opinion, is weird, or someone who we should take a closer look at. We need to know who paid for the room, what name it's in and every piece of camera footage from the moment the guest walked through the doors. Oh, and we're also going to need to go back up there and speak to everyone on that floor."

He sighed but nodded. Then he curled a finger and beckoned them to follow him into the back office. Nearby a receptionist was fussing over an elderly couple seated on two of the tired, velvet armchairs near to the elevator. "Shanice, keep an eye on the desk and if you see Mr. Lord come back in, tell him I need to speak to him."

She beamed. "Yes, sir." Then she turned back to the waiting couple.

The back room was spacious—or it would have been if it wasn't for rows of filing cabinets that filled the entire length of one wall.

"You have almost as many files as we do." Maria smiled at him, and he nodded.

"I like to keep detailed records of the guests. Repeat guests get their own file so I can make sure they get everything they need."

"That's pretty sweet of you. Is that what the upper management expect you to do?"

He laughed and his eyes crinkled at the corners, making Maria warm to him more than she'd first expected. "The upper management don't care; they want the rooms full and the money flowing. They don't particularly care about giving guests a five-star service at a three-star hotel."

"But you do?"

"I do. If someone pays good money to stay here, then I want to make sure they get value for their bucks. How else do you think we keep pulling in the guests? They might go on Tripadvisor and write that the hotel is a shithole, that it needs a facelift, but they can't fault the service or the staff, and the value for money far exceeds expectations."

Frankie nodded. "That's good business sense."

"I think so."

Maria smiled at him. "What about the long-term rentals? Do you treat them the same as the guests?" This had absolutely nothing to do with their investigation, but she was interested to know.

"Of course. They are our fixed income and also deserve the very best service available to them for the money they pay."

His whole attitude was refreshing. Maria realized he would have helped them even without the little talk Frankie gave him.

"Are there any guests or residents stopping here at the moment that you think could have killed those girls? Anyone who gives off bad vibes, weird vibes? I'm pretty sure you know the kind of people I'm talking about. The ones who you speak to and think there's something not right with them."

Rick paused. "There are a few residents that do give me pause for thought. I wouldn't want to go back to their rooms with them because they're kind of creepy. But it doesn't mean they killed those girls. Do you crap where you eat, is my question?"

"I would have to say no, definitely not. But some people are wired a little differently to the rest of us and wouldn't think twice about crapping on the table before eating their Thanksgiving dinner from it."

Rick threw back his head and laughed. "Yeah, I guess so. We do have a guy on the tenth who is a bit strange, wears a trilby, never takes it off, and always has it pulled down over his eyes. He also still wears a face mask, even though most of us gave them up when they declared Covid was no longer a threat. He sometimes brings girls back with him and there is no way he's picked them up legitimately."

"Hookers?" asked Frankie.

"I prefer the term ladies of the night, but yeah, he definitely pays them by the hour. But I don't know if that makes him a killer."

Maria shrugged. "Probably not, but we're going to need to check him out. What room is he in?"

"1003, Mr. Farquet, and please don't tell him I suggested you check him out."

"We won't—we're discreet, aren't we, Frankie? If you could get the guest list sent over to my email, that would be great, and the download of the footage. I'd really appreciate it."

"Of course. Let me just check who paid for the room for you."

They waited while Rick logged onto the ancient computer that looked like it belonged in a museum. He shook his head at the screen and then shrugged. "Well, that's strange. According to this, nobody has rented that room since last week. It should be empty. Yes, oh damn, I forgot, what with everything going on and having to evacuate the hotel. It's the room that had a major leak. The tub leaks straight out onto the floor. Maintenance were going to take a look at it tomorrow."

Maria glanced at Frankie. "Who would have known about this and who would have access to the room?"

"Well, maintenance knew about it, the maids, the concierge, everyone who works here would have known it wasn't available until the plumbers had been in."

"Then we're going to need a full staff list, too, and the names of any outside contractors you have spoken to about it. What about the guests, would they have known?"

Rick shook his head. "I can't see how they would." He brought up the lists and documents to add to a file. "What's your email? I'll get these sent over now. The film footage will take a while because I have to get onto the system, which is ancient, and log in, then try to download it onto this beast of a machine before I can send it."

Maria rattled off her email, watching him write it down on the legal pad by the side of the keyboard to make sure he got it right. "What about staff? Do you employ anyone here who kind of gives you the creeps, bad vibes, the kind of person you give a wide berth to?"

He shrugged. "It takes all sorts of people to run and maintain a hotel, detective. If there was anyone I thought might fit that description, then I wouldn't be trusting them to have free rein of the building."

"Okay. Can we speak with the maids for that floor?"

"Yes, take a seat and I'll go downstairs and see if I can find them. There are two of them and they're waiting patiently along with a couple of others to go clean up the mess out in the hallway. Obviously, the room is out of service until you give the go ahead for them to go in."

He left them sitting there and Frankie whispered, "What do you think about him?"

"He seems okay, helpful. I'm not getting any weird vibes from him. You?"

"Yeah, I think he's okay. Helpful, too, which makes a change."

They watched people come and go. Tiffany passed them on the way out to the van to load the samples. A couple of crime scene techs they didn't know also came down with brown paper sacks. There was a cop stationed outside the crime scene, as would probably be the case for the foreseeable future, or until they decided to move the bodies. It all depended on how long the CSI techs took. They had the whole hallway to search, not to mention the lifts and stairwells. It could take a couple of hours at least.

Loud voices from somewhere in the foyer filtered through to them.

"I told you it was a bad omen. Every single time I see her something terrible happens."

"Shush, dear. You're being too loud, and people are listening."

Maria stood up, interested to see who was talking, and saw two women in their sixties. Both wore black suits and carried purses over their shoulders. Maria knew vintage Chanel when she saw it and nodded appreciatively. Missy, her next-door neighbor and dear friend, had a collection that never failed to impress her.

"I don't care what people say. Whenever I see her, it means someone is about to croak it."

"If you carry on being so loud, it will be you, because I'll strangle you myself."

This made Maria chuckle, and she walked towards them. Tugging out her badge, she held it up.

"Good evening, ladies. Detective Maria Miller. Could I speak to you for a minute?"

They looked at her, eyes wide and mouths agape. "Of course, how can we help, detective?"

Maria pointed to a couple of vacant chairs, and they all sat down.

"I'm sorry, I couldn't help but overhear your conversation." The woman with cropped platinum hair glared at her friend with a knowing look. Her friend looked away. "I didn't catch your names."

The other woman, who had hair as dark as Maria's, smiled at her. "I'm Angeline, this is my sister Josephine, but most people call us Angie and Jo."

"Such pretty names. Are you staying here on vacation?"

Jo laughed. "Honey, we live here. I'd like to think if I was on vacation, I'd choose something a little more, shall we say, upmarket."

Maria found it strange the sisters would live somewhere like this. They seemed to her like they'd be more suited to a life uptown.

Angie leaned closer. "The rent is cheaper here; it means we can still do lunch every day and shop till we drop when we feel like it, and Jo here has never been very comfortable staying anywhere too posh. She loves to slum it." Jo glared at her, but Angie didn't seem to notice.

"What did you mean when you said that whenever you saw her something bad happens? I assume you've heard about the murders up on the thirteenth floor?"

Angie threw her hands up in the air. "I told you, you're always too loud, Jo."

Jo rolled her eyes at her sister, then turned to Maria. "And she's always too dramatic. It was nothing, really."

"I won't say anything to your neighbors, but I really want to know who you were talking about."

"I don't know how familiar you are with this place, but there's a rumor that a woman in blue haunts the tenth floor.

Apparently, she was staying here with her daughter—they had an argument and she decided to cut off her own hand, then jump out of the window. Lord knows why she would put herself through that kind of agony when she was going to throw herself out of the window, but she did, and now she's stuck here in some kind of purgatory."

Maria felt icy chills run all the way down from the back of her neck to the base of her spine and she shuddered. "Bless her, that's awful, and her poor daughter, too."

Angie shrugged. "Maybe the daughter was a complete bitch and drove her to it. Not all kids are as innocent as we think they are. Besides, she was an adult, not a child."

"Why did you say that people croak it when they see her?"

Jo stared at Maria. "You saw her, too, didn't you? When?"

"I thought I saw someone in blue, only for a split second, when we arrived."

Jo glanced at Angie. "Honey, I don't want to be the bearer of bad news but whenever I see her, someone dies."

That cold shiver spread from the base of Maria's spine outwards, covering her arms in goosebumps.

Angie shook her head. "Take no notice of her, she's superstitious and full of crap."

Jo ignored her sister. "It doesn't mean it's someone you know. Look, I saw her this morning when I walked into the hallway. She was standing there, all shimmering and mist-like with her back to me, staring out of the window down at the street. She was probably there because of those poor girls. She's a bit like one of those old-fashioned weather barometers, only instead of announcing it's going to rain, she announces a death."

Maria didn't feel any better. Rick came hurrying towards them with the two maids he'd gone looking for. He glanced at Maria, Angie and Jo.

"Good evening, ladies. How are you both today?"

Angie smiled. "Good evening, Rick. We'd be a hell of a lot better if you didn't let women get murdered in here."

His cheeks turned a vivid shade of red and he nodded. "You're right about that. Please know that we will be upping security and if you see anything you are worried about, then let me know."

Jo answered. "We will, darling, thank you."

He looked at Maria. "Rosa and Melody are ready for you."

"Thank you."

He hurried towards the office, and Maria stood up. "Have either of you noticed anyone strange hanging around the hotel? Have you seen anything suspicious?" They shook their heads and said no in perfect unison. "Well, thank you."

As she walked away Maria couldn't shake the chill in her bones, or the ominous feeling of dread that had settled in the pit of her stomach.

SEVEN

He didn't hurry when he left the hotel. He never hurried. Life was generally all hustle and bustle in this city, and he was tired of it. He practically slowed down to a snail's pace to allow himself time to think, because he needed plenty of time to do that.

The cool bag was tucked inside the heavy satchel in his left hand. He had to swap it to his right hand, and back again. Who knew feet could weigh so much? He supposed they were a dead weight. He laughed at his own joke, though he knew nobody else would find it funny. He didn't care what other people thought. Not anymore. He'd lost everything and had been about to end it all when he'd been sent to the Parker, and his life had changed overnight.

He'd been working on the hotel's water tower by himself when he'd heard the voice. At first, he thought it was the breeze blowing through the gap in the door, and turned around every couple of minutes to check. Then it got a little louder and he wondered if someone was outside on the rooftop calling to him. He'd downed tools to go and check, but the rooftop had been empty. Puzzled, he chalked it up to one of those things. He hadn't been sleeping too good since Chloe walked out on him, taking just about everything except the bed, a coffee cup, a set of cutlery for one and a single towel. The bitch had cleared out everything.

After thinking about her, he had to stop and breathe deeply for a few moments to bring the anger back down to a reasonable level. Then he carried on trying to fix the broken door. The lock had been ripped clean off and the hinges had come away, leaving the tower accessible to anyone. Since that incident at the hotel where a girl was found in a water tank, most reputable hotels kept on top of that kind of maintenance.

He heard the deep voice as clear as day once the door was fixed closed. It scared him because it was dark inside the tower, and he knew there was only him inside. He'd called out in case some homeless dude was sleeping up there, perhaps the reason the door was broken in the first place. They might have kicked it in to get out of the cold. But there was no answer. It was colder than a witch's tit inside the tower. If he were homeless, he'd rather take his chances out on the streets or a park bench rather than stay inside this deep, dark, eerie place.

After he'd first heard the voice, he started looking into the history of the hotel. He joined some ghost hunting groups online to see if that stuff was real or if he was hallucinating. It turned out the Parker had quite a following of ghost enthusiasts. He found himself reading about it for hours, lost in the tales of spooky happenings and murders. That led to him to start offering ghost hunters the chance to take a peek inside the most infamous haunted room of them all, room 1303.

There was a profit to be made; he could give tours of the room for fifty bucks an hour when it was vacant. Meanwhile, the voice got steadily worse. The craving to kill took over, even though he'd never been a violent man before working in the Parker. Then there were the bad dreams. He often woke in a cold sweat in the early hours of the morning, alone and terrified of what that voice would say to him when it whispered in his ear. He knew then that he was haunted by something dark. The only way to appease it was to do exactly as it told him. That way it might leave him alone. It wanted him to bring fresh victims to the hotel, so it could gather the strength to come back from whatever purgatory it was stuck in. He'd always been a sucker for a sob story.

The bag was heavy. He had to keep checking the sidewalk to make sure it wasn't dripping blood, even though he'd wrapped the feet in towels first. He would keep them at home until it was safe to put them where they belonged. He wasn't brave enough to go to the tower with them yet, in case he got caught. How would he explain that to the cops or any of the other hotel staff?

Maybe then the voice would leave him alone. Maybe it would stop burying itself into the depths of his head where he couldn't shake it free. He wasn't a killer. He was sad, lonely and pissed about Chloe's sudden disappearing act, but never, ever before had he felt the urge to go pick up a couple of teenage runaways, strangle them and remove their feet. Just the thought of what he'd done made him feel sick to the bottom of his stomach. He needed to lie down in a dark room and sleep. Sleeping would help him forget what he'd done to them.

The horror on their faces when they'd realized he wasn't being kind by offering them somewhere to stay so they could hunt for ghosts... The cute one, Dory, had known before her friend what was happening. But by then it was too late. As the roofies kicked in, and they'd become all sluggish and unresponsive, there was a moment when Dory had murmured, "No, please don't hurt us." And boy, had he felt bad. Like a real asshole. He'd changed his mind and apologized to them, muttering "sorry" over and over again as he'd dragged their heavy bodies onto the twin beds in room 1303.

As he'd sat on the chair watching them, he wondered if he

could just leave them like that. Let them wake up with a hangover from hell, unsure what had happened. They'd still be breathing, and they could carry on with their lives. Maybe go on to settle down and have families of their own someday. The voice didn't like that idea. It hissed at him to do it, to kill them and bring it their feet. He'd given in because he'd been afraid.

And now look at the mess he was in.

EIGHT

Maids Rosa and Melody both looked as if they'd rather be any place than here. Straight backed with grim expressions, they were sitting on the chairs that Maria and Frankie had occupied minutes before. Frankie kept smiling at them and Maria wasn't sure if he was freaking them out. She introduced them both to the women, who still looked scared.

"We just want to ask you some questions about the room where the bodies were found. You're not in any trouble at all."

Melody side-eyed Rosa, whose hands were clasped tightly in her lap. It was Melody who took the lead. "What do you want to know?"

"Did you see anyone go into that room? Notice it was occupied, hear or see anything that you might have thought was strange but didn't think anything more of it?"

Before she could answer, Shanice called, "Hey, Rickie, Mr. Lord just came in—should I call him over?"

Rick stood up. "Excuse me, I need to talk to him." He walked out, leaving Rosa looking even more startled than before. Melody reached out and patted her hand.

"That room is strange, always has been since I started working here ten years ago."

"How is it strange?"

"Things turn on by themselves, the faucets run when it's empty, the lights flicker. The door sometimes sticks, and you can't turn the handle, no matter how hard you pull it. It's cold in there, too, always cold, even with the heating on full."

Rosa nodded and crossed herself. Maria found it fascinating that she was obviously more scared of that room than the pair of police officers questioning her.

"We don't go in there on our own, do we, Rosa? We go in together. At one point I used to, but the strange things began to get worse and then I was off sick. Rosa had to get it cleaned up ready for the next guests and the door got stuck. She couldn't get out of there; the lights were flicking on and off and the faucet was pouring with water."

Rosa rocked back and forth, her palms pressed together in a prayer position.

"We told the manager, and he said we were not to go in there on our own, that it was okay to work together in that room. He also said the door should be propped wide open, so we don't get stuck in there again. It's an awful, awful room."

Rosa whispered in Spanish. "La maldad, el diablo."

Maria answered her. "You think the room is evil? That the devil is inside it, Rosa?"

Frankie looked as if he was going to walk right out of the office. Maria silently pleaded with him to stay put.

Rosa nodded. "Yes, ma'am. Something is bad inside it. I hear the scratching. It lives inside the walls and now look what happened."

"Does Rick believe this, too? After you got stuck in there, he agreed with you?"

"Not Mr. Rick. It was Mr. Stanley. This happened a few years ago."

Maria changed tack. "How about this week, have you seen anybody going in or out?"

Both women shrugged and Melody answered. "Maintenance were in and out. They realized they needed a plumber but ours is on holiday—he's back next week."

"Who's maintenance?"

"Billy, Buzz and Zane. There's three of them work full time and a couple of contractors who come in and help out when needed."

Maria pulled out her notepad and scribbled their names down. She needed to check them against the list Rick had emailed her and find out who the contractors were.

"When was the last time you were inside the room?"

Melody counted on her fingers. "Five days ago. The last guest checked out complaining it was too cold in there and the tub was leaking. We went in, changed the beds, mopped up the mess and put towels down to soak up the water. Told Rickie about it and haven't been back in since."

"Did you see those girls go into the room, see who they were with?"

Rosa shook her head. Melody did, too. "Nope, we finish by three and start at seven. They had to have come in after three. That room is right next to the supply cupboard—we'd have noticed anyone going in and out. I'm sorry we can't be any more help than that."

"Don't be sorry. That's great. Means we can narrow down a timeline as to when they came into the hotel. Thank you for speaking to us."

Rosa stood up. "We are free to go, yes?"

"Absolutely."

Melody was out of the office first, closely followed by Rosa, who turned back to look at Maria. She slipped a rosary bead from around her neck and held out her hand towards her. Maria smiled at her but shook her head. "No, it's okay, thank you. You keep that, Rosa. What makes you think I need it?"

She pushed it further towards Maria. "You need to take care of yourself. You have been inside that room and seen the awful things. This hotel... it's not what it seems. Bad things happen when you least expect it. Keep it, I have plenty more at home."

Maria took the beads, not wanting to insult her, and smiled. "Thank you." Rosa nodded then hurried after Melody, leaving Maria feeling more than a little perturbed. Frankie began to snigger.

"Boy, you do attract them."

She turned to him. "What, weird people or evil spirits?"

Still laughing, he replied, "Both."

Maria gave him the finger but pushed the beads into her trouser pocket. If the maids thought this place was evil and the guests saw the ghost of a woman in blue, who was she to disregard it? She'd done that before and look where it had gotten her. No, Maria was cautious after everything she'd been through, and if Rosa thought that she needed a little protection from God, then so be it. She would accept it gratefully and hope this was nothing more cut and dried than a cold, cruel killer. Nothing remotely supernatural.

"I guess it's time to go door knock up on the thirteenth floor, and then maybe we can grab something to eat. Do you know how hungry I am?"

Frankie stared at her, and she nodded. "Let's do it and yes, I'm aware that you are starving."

At the mention of food, her phone pinged, and she glanced down to see a message from Harrison. "Late supper?"

After she finished here, she could either go home on her own and sit there feeling all creeped out, or she could go home, get changed and spend a couple of hours being wined and dined with Harrison.

Yes, pick me up in ninety minutes from home. X

Frankie didn't ask who she was texting. By the expression on his face, he already knew. She could ask him if he wanted to come. Harrison was the kind of guy who wouldn't be bothered if he did, and would still insist on paying for all three of them. But she needed a break from Frankie. They'd been together for almost ten hours already. It was worse than being married. The commitment it took to being partnered up with someone was huge, not to mention time consuming. They practically lived in and out of each other's pockets.

It would be fun to have a couple of hours where she didn't have to think about work. Not that she would forget those two girls; they were a part of her now, tucked away in the piece of her mind where she stored information on the victims she'd worked to find justice for. As sad as it was, life did go on. If she was to put her all into finding their killer, a couple of hours to give her mind time to breathe wasn't going to make any difference to anyone but her own mental health.

NINE

Showered, her thick, black hair scraped back into a sleek chignon, she slipped on the plain, black cocktail dress with the scooped neckline and lace sleeves that Missy had insisted she take from her wardrobe and wear. Both of them pretended the Dior label inside wasn't there because Maria had fallen in love with its cut and simplicity. Missy was adamant that she had no use for it and it suited Maria far better than it had ever suited her.

Maria checked two diamond studs were still in her ears, slipped on a couple of the bracelets that Harrison had also bought her, and stared at her limited choice of shoes. She'd a couple of pairs of heels but didn't enjoy wearing them. They served their purpose. But despite her best efforts, she was still tired after a long day, so opted for a pair of pumps that wouldn't make her feet ache after ten minutes.

There was a knock on her door. Wrapping the soft, black cashmere pashmina around her shoulders, she peered through the peephole to see Harrison on the other side, grinning at her. Opening the door, he stared, his mouth open.

"What are you looking at?"

"You. You know you're beautiful, don't you?"

Maria threw back her head and laughed. Her fingers reached up to pat the streak of white hair and make sure it was still in place where it should be.

"You know flattery will get you everywhere."

"I'm serious, Maria, you truly are beautiful. Thank you for agreeing to be my date tonight, I've been thinking about you nonstop all day. I almost didn't message because I thought you'd say no and my heart couldn't take it, but I had to see you, and I'm glad I did."

Heat rose in her cheeks and they turned pink. "You're actually a pretty sweet guy, you know. Or is this some ploy to get me drunk and into bed?" She laughed, but she was hoping that it was. She hoped that tonight she wouldn't have to come home on her own.

She took in his black suit, white shirt, gold cufflinks, the contours of his face that looked even more chiseled than the last time she'd seen him, and leaned forward until she was close enough that she could brush her lips against his. This took him by surprise, but only for a second, then he pulled her close, their lips pressing against each other.

"Get a room, the pair of you."

They pulled apart to see Missy standing inside the elevator with a case. Maria smiled as Missy walked out into the hallway.

"Don't stop on my account. I don't want to be the one to get in the way of love's young dream."

Maria felt a little relieved at the interruption. It helped the heat that had overtaken her body to cool off slightly.

"I thought you were on vacation. Where's Emilia?"

"Getting food. You know when you get to my age if the bed isn't comfortable there is no point suffering on any longer. It's just not worth the aches and pains. And Emilia has been complaining about her arm aching a lot lately. She needs to go see a physiotherapist. Then again, at our age, everything aches. We'd had enough and decided to come back home. My hips just can't take hard beds anymore. But enough about me. I'm old, I'm supposed to be in pain. Look at the pair of you, beautiful humans. You know it makes my heart happy to see you both looking so in love. Have I ever told you that life's too short to not do what your heart tells you to?" She arched an eyebrow at Maria.

Maria smiled. "Lots of times."

"Well, I'm happy to see you take notice. Don't be like me and spend all your time wishing you'd listened. Go, have fun, and wild, hot sex, too."

Harrison's cheeks turned a deep red, but he chuckled. Maria grabbed Missy's case and as Missy opened her door, rolled it inside and pecked her cheek before leaving.

"I mean it, have a wonderful evening."

"You too, Missy."

Back in the hallway, Harrison was waiting by the lift with a grin on his face.

"I like Missy's advice." He winked at Maria, who shook her head.

"Yeah, I bet you do. So, where are we going? I hope to God they have food, proper food, not that three carrot sticks with a drizzle of honey and one tiny chunk of steak that wouldn't fill a child, never mind an adult."

"I thought we could try Luca's and grab some pizza before I sweep you off your feet and take you to the Plaza where my cousin is having her birthday party."

"Are there going to be cocktails at some point?"

"Of course."

"Fine, feed me the best pizza in New York then I'll try to be polite to your family."

He laughed. "Don't worry about the family, they'll be drunk by the time we get there and won't really be interested in anything other than a good old fight. You'll be pleased to know my mom is out of town, so you're safe."

Maria laughed. "I like your mom; she only wants what's best for you. You're her son, I get that. If I had kids, I would be the same. I wouldn't want my only son throwing his life away with some tough broad who chases killers and Lord knows what else all day through the streets of New York."

His fingers reached out to stroke her cheek. "You wouldn't, huh?"

"Nope."

"Well, it's a good job that I don't listen to either of you. I love you, Maria Miller, whether you love me or not. You stole my heart the day you shot that perp in the leg and left him bleeding all over my brand-new marble flooring."

"You're even more screwed up than I realized."

He laughed. "Probably, but you make me happier than any woman I've ever dated. You also make me hornier than any of them, too, so maybe you could cut me some slack now and again and not be so hard on me."

They walked out into the cool night air. There was a bite to the cold that made Maria's hot cheeks instantly cool down. She was grateful because she knew if he'd kissed her again, they wouldn't have got this far out of the building. She would have dragged him back inside and straight into her bed. He opened the door of the Mercedes for her, and she smiled at the driver.

"Evening, Maria. It's great to see you."

"Good evening, Lenny, it's great to see you, too."

Harrison sat next to her, and she felt her whole body relax as she sank back into the soft, leather seat. He smelled so good and looked even better. She wrapped her fingers around his and stared out of the window. She saw the smile on his lips in the reflection and decided that she was going to cut him a lot of slack. Despite her intentions, she knew she was falling in love with him and that made her happier than she ever imagined she could be. Missy and Emilia would be overjoyed when she admitted this to them. Maria might finally accept that it was possible to fall in love with someone way out of her league.

As they walked into Luca's pizzeria and the smell of freshly baked dough and melted mozzarella hit her nostrils, Maria felt her shoulders finally relax for the first time in hours. She hadn't forgotten about the two girls, but she was no good to them if she didn't eat, let her brain rest and get some sleep. Tomorrow was a new day; she would get an early start and do everything possible to find the creep that killed them. Tonight, she needed a cocktail or two to help her unwind and unknot the feeling of unease building inside her ever since she caught a glimpse of that woman staring down at her from up on the tenth floor of the Parker.

TEN

Maria's breath was a smoky white mist that plumed in the air. The thirteenth floor was far colder than it should be for a hotel. It was also much darker than she remembered it being yesterday. She glanced up at the rusted chandeliers to see if the bulbs had been removed or if they were just out. Still in place, the bulbs flickered. Stepping into the lift, the doors closed behind her. She knew she shouldn't have come up here on her own. What the hell was she thinking? This place was watching her. The whole building was a living, breathing entity and the fear she'd felt since yesterday was bubbling up inside her, almost at boiling point.

There was no one around. Yellow and black police tape crisscrossed the soot-stained door to room 1303. The door wasn't shut tight, which infuriated her. How goddamn hard was it to make sure the room was locked behind the last person out of there? Anyone could have gone inside. There were always people with a morbid sense of curiosity everywhere you went. They could have gone in and taken bedding, towels, anything they could sell on eBay to the ghouls who collected stuff like that. There was a market for it. Buyers paid good prices. Maria had no idea why anyone would want the bloodstained sheets of a murder victim in their home, but she knew that people did.

Frankie was late, and now she was going to have to go into that room alone. For a hotel with guests, she found this place unnaturally still. Even the elevator wasn't going up and down; the machinery was deadly silent. She didn't want to do this, but someone was going to have to. It always seemed to be her. But Maria's feet felt like two balls of lead. They didn't want to move, which she took as a bad sign. Forcing them forward, she moved in slow motion, glad that Frankie wasn't here to laugh at her— although she probably wouldn't be as freaked out if he was.

There was no warmth or life to this place, not like there was at the Plaza. Maria smiled. Last night had been a blast and Harrison was a pretty smooth dancer. His young cousin was beautiful and fun. Maria had taken an instant shine to the teenage girl. She thought about the fact that they'd danced until her feet ached and how glad she'd been to be so exhausted when she'd fallen into bed next to Harrison last night.

As she walked towards the room in what felt like slow motion, the dim bulbs that lit the corridor began to pop, one by one, plunging her into darkness. She stifled a screech by cupping the palm of her hand over her mouth. Her heart raced. She needed to get a grip on herself; she was letting this place get to her. The only light was from the fire exit signs. Maria knew she should turn around and leave, go straight down to the reception area and wait for Frankie to turn up.

Movement in the corner of her eye made her turn to see a shadow of what looked like a man, not much taller than her and stocky.

"Hey, who is that? What's up with the lights? There must be some kind of electrical fault."

There was no answer. Maria was almost at the door but could still see the shadowy figure at the other end of the hall. She had a bad feeling that whoever was just out of sight was waiting for her next move. A low chuckle filled the air, the creepiest sound she'd ever heard, sending her survival senses into overdrive. The shadow moved but she didn't see who it could belong to. It made the tiny hairs on the back of her neck bristle, and she turned to return to the elevators. If she could have reached the stairs, she'd have taken her chance and run, but they were in the direction of whoever the freak was trying to scare her.

Sudden pounding footsteps running towards her kicked her into action. She sprinted towards the elevator. Glancing behind her, she saw the shadow run along the wall. Maria slammed her hand against the call button, praying the lift would get here before the shadow thing reached her. The doors slid silently open, and she darted inside. But not before she felt a sharp, burning sensation against her shoulder blade. She stared in the mirror inside the elevator and saw that the back of her shoulder had a deep, bleeding scratch.

Opening her mouth, she let out a scream. It was so loud it jolted her out of the restless sleep she'd been in. Harrison, who was next to her in the Plaza bed, jumped upright.

"Hey, it's okay, it's just a bad dream. You were having a nightmare; everything is okay now, Maria."

He reached out to stroke her arm and she threw his hand away. "Turn on the lights, now."

He jumped up and bathed the room in light, banishing the shadows from the corners. She was out of breath. Beads of perspiration were all over her brow as she threw the covers off and ran into the bathroom, slamming the door shut behind her.

Maria was freaking out. It was just a bad dream. She stared at her reflection in the bathroom mirror—the rear of her shoulder burned and she felt an intense wave of terror wash over her. She wasn't sure she could take a peek. Breathing deeply to calm herself down a little, she turned slowly and saw the angry red gash. It had to have been caused by something razor sharp slicing into her shoulder blade.

For the first time in forever, she wanted to cry. She felt so afraid, because although she'd been dreaming, whatever had happened to her was real, whether she was really on the thirteenth floor in the Parker or in Harrison's suite at the Plaza. Something or someone—and she had no idea what had chased her down the hallway—had tried to stab her.

With shaking hands, she turned on the faucet and ran a washcloth under it. She wanted to clean the wound before it could get infected, only she couldn't reach. There was a gentle knock on the door.

"Maria, are you okay in there?"

"I'm fine, just give me a minute."

She stared at the angry wound in the mirror. It needed disinfecting. "Actually, could you come in here, please?"

Harrison walked in and gasped at the state of her shoulder. "How did you do that? You must have caught it on the mattress. Maybe there's a spring poking through. Jesus. Maria, that looks painful."

She felt a little of the tension she was holding drain away. Of course. There had to be a rational explanation. She probably had caught it on a spring or something sharp and tore it tossing and turning.

"Could you bathe it for me? I don't want it to get infected."

"Of course, but I think it might need to be looked at. Let me call a paramedic I know. He'll come and check it out."

She shook her head. "No, it just needs cleaning up. Is there a first aid kit somewhere?"

Only Harrison would have a paramedic on call at his disposal. She didn't tease him about it; as much as she liked the rogue spring theory, she was still too afraid that the dream had caused her injury.

He went back into the bedroom and dialed the concierge,

requesting the manager and a first aid kit to attend his suite immediately. Maria wanted to tell him to stop causing a fuss, but if there was something dangerous sticking out of the mattress, it needed fixing before someone else caught themselves.

Moments later there was a knock on the door and Harrison let the manager in. He pointed to Maria's shoulder. "Henry, look what happened while we were in bed. There must be something sharp sticking out of the mattress. I want it replacing immediately."

"Mr. Williams, I'm so sorry. I will get maintenance to bring a brand-new replacement immediately. Ms. Miller, can I get you some medical assistance to take care of your shoulder?"

She shook her head, feeling stupid and more than a little embarrassed with all the fuss. "The first aid kit will be fine, thank you."

Henry handed the box to Harrison, who came back into the bathroom, closing the door behind him.

"I'm not too bad at patching up. Sit on the edge of the tub and I'll sort you out."

"Thank you, I feel like such an idiot."

He bent down and kissed her forehead. "You are many things, but an idiot is not one of them. Now, grit your teeth because this might sting."

He uncapped a bottle of iodine and tipped it out onto a piece of gauze, then pressed it against the deep cut, making Maria groan a little. She bit her lip to stop herself making any further noise. She kept telling herself it was okay—there was a faulty spring, and it was just a scratch, but deep down she feared that it wasn't okay at all.

Something living inside the Parker Hotel had tried to kill her while she was dreaming, like some kind of Freddy Krueger boogey man.

ELEVEN

With all the fuss and the hotel staff coming in and out, Maria tugged on her clothes. After Harrison had dressed her injury, he grabbed her hand and pulled her out of the room, still in his robe and slippers. "Come on, it's like Times Square in here. Let's go get a drink."

She didn't argue with him. A shot of something strong might help soothe the churning inside her stomach. Harrison led her out into the brightly lit hallway. Though it looked nothing like the thirteenth floor in the Parker, she hoped to God there wasn't a door with crisscrossed crime scene tape over it. How cruel that would be to have a nightmare inside a nightmare. She poked him in the side, then pinched the skin on her arm.

"Ouch, what's that for. Why did you poke me?"

"Sorry. I needed to check I wasn't still stuck in that dream."

He smiled at her, squeezing her fingers gently. "Definitely not dreaming, unless we're both in the same dream. It was that bad, huh?" She nodded. "You scared me. Do you want to talk about it? Might make you feel better while it's still fresh in your mind."

The hotel was deserted except for the desk staff and mainte-nance crew, who replaced bulbs in one of the huge cut-glass chandeliers. Harrison led her to the champagne bar, which was bathed in the warm glow of the many lamps positioned around the room. It felt so strange to be sitting at the marble bar, just the two of them at... She realized she had no idea what time it was. "Do you know what time it is?"

Harrison flicked his wrist. The diamonds encrusted in the face of the Rolex he was wearing sparkled in the light. "Three thirty."

"Thanks."

One of the desk staff came in. "Can I help you, Mr. Williams?"

"We'd like a drink of something to help us sleep. Do you recommend anything in particular?"

The guy smiled at him. "I'm not much of a bartender, but I think a shot of something strong and smooth might help. How about Rémy Martin or Martell?" He was pointing to the row of expensive bottles.

Maria shook her head. "I don't like brandy. Grey Goose will do just fine, thank you."

Harrison smiled. "Grey Goose it is. Do you want to just leave us the bottle and two glasses? We can serve ourselves."

"Of course, Mr. Williams."

He passed them an almost full bottle of vodka, filled up an ice bucket and placed it next to them with two beautiful, crystal tumblers. "Will there be anything else, sir?"

"No, thank you, Jack."

Jack gave a little bow and left them to it. Maria watched as Harrison scooped some ice into the glasses, uncapped the vodka and poured a generous amount into both. He passed one to her and she took it, saying, "Za nas."

He nodded, lifted his glass and replied, "Yes, to us."

They both tipped back their heads and took a huge gulp of

the neat vodka. Maria relished the warmth as the cold liquid soothed the back of her throat and instantly began to thaw her frozen insides. Harrison coughed, and she grinned at him.

"It takes a little practice."

He nodded. "How did you learn to drink like a hard-core Soviet?"

"There's a Russian bar on 52nd Street. Viktor the bar manager showed me how."

"Was he your boyfriend?"

She laughed. "Sadly not. He works there, and when I had to go there on inquiries, he offered me a drink. It seemed rude not to accept."

"You are a woman of many mysteries, Maria. I know the bar. Before all the trouble, I had a business associate who would only meet there. I often wonder how he is. He went home to take care of his family."

Maria realized that she knew nothing about Harrison's business associates or how he ran his business and decided that she'd rather keep it that way. It would blow her mind.

"So, do you want to talk about your nightmare? I've never seen you looking so shaken or scared and I'm not going to lie, you scared me. I didn't realize that the beautiful, tough Detective Miller could feel that way." He placed his hand on top of hers. "I kind of liked being your protector for all of sixty seconds."

She laughed. "Gee, I guess you got a peep under this thick rhinoceros hide I wear and saw that I'm a flesh and blood woman beneath."

"I saw a woman who was terrified, Maria. I'm not joking, you scared me. I thought there was someone in the room with us."

"Now, that would have been fine. I can deal with living, breathing things I can see with my eyes open." She paused, not sure she wanted to tell him what had happened, though a part of her did. If she couldn't share moments like this, what was the point of being with him?

"I was back on the thirteenth floor of the Parker where the girls were killed. It was dark. Someone had been in the room where the double murder happened, and I saw the shadow of a guy against the wall. It chased me to the lift. It was fast for a shadow. The whole time it was laughing and then I felt a sharp, burning pain, and woke up next to you with my shoulder a mess."

She watched his face to see if he was going to laugh at her, but he didn't.

"That is terrifying."

"Yeah, tell me about it."

"I don't know what to say. Did you think it was real?"

She nodded. "I've seen some stuff the last few months that would turn your hair white. It's certainly turned mine that way. Stuff I would never, ever in a billion years believe if I hadn't seen it with my own eyes. The kind of stuff that has had me questioning my sanity. Frankie has seen it, too, or most of it. He can back me up. I'm not crazy. There is stuff out there that we have no concept of, things that would scare us to death if we let them."

She stopped talking and poured out another measure of vodka, drinking it straight down. This time the heat reached all the way to her churning stomach, instantly calming the knots of anxiety.

"Maybe it's time to consider a change of career, take up something that won't scare you to death or give you bad dreams."

She laughed. "Like what? I'm a born and bred cop, Harrison, I don't know how to do anything else."

"What would you do if you could do anything in the world, nothing to stop you?"

She closed her eyes and thought about what she'd love to do if she could, then opened them. "Homicide detective."

He laughed. "That doesn't count. You are already one of those, and a fine one, too."

"I don't know. I've never thought about it. Write crime stories, learn how to bake fancy biscuits, open a bookshop with a little café and read all day."

"I can make any of those things happen. I know you struggle with the difference in wealth between us and I understand my lifestyle can be a bit of a shock. But, what's the point in having lots of bucks if you can't put it to good use? I can help you by financing you to open the bookshop and café. It's not charity. It would be a full-on business arrangement; I would want a cut of the profits and a business plan from you to know that it could work. But between us, we can make it happen. Do you know how happy I would be to see you doing something that made you smile and didn't turn your hair white or see you get hurt?

"And before you go thinking it means you would be tied to me forever, it wouldn't. I love you, Maria, I want you to be happy and I want you in my life whether we're together or not. I never want to lose you as a friend. Yes, I would marry you in a heartbeat. If I thought you'd say yes, I'd whisk you off to some tropical island and marry you on a beach, just the pair of us and a couple of locals to witness it. But I know that's not what you want and I'm okay with that."

"I think the vodka has gone to your head."

"No, you have gone to my head and it's not a bad thing. I just figured while we're being open with each other I'd let you know the depth of my feelings and how far I'm willing to go."

Tears pricked at the corner of her eyes; she swiped them away with her sleeve.

"Is that you proposing to me?"

He smiled. "Absolutely not, Miller. I'm just saying that I'd be willing to do anything to make you happy."

"Thank you, it means a lot to me and one day I might just take you up on that offer."

His eyes looked hopeful. "Which one?"

"Both of them, but just not at the moment. I know I'm a pain in the ass, but I have a job to do. Two teenage girls were brutally murdered yesterday and whether I have bad dreams or not, I have to find their killer. I don't expect you to understand that, but it's who I am."

He leaned forwards, pulling her towards him, kissed her, then let her go.

"And that's why I love you. The world is a much safer, better place with you in it, Maria, and when you're ready to discuss your options, I'll be waiting for you."

A gentle cough at the door made them both turn to see the manager.

"Sorry to interrupt, Mr. Williams. The bed is ready for you. The mattress has been replaced and it's been made up ready for you both. Once again, I'm sorry you got hurt, Miss Miller, and if you want to file a report against the hotel then I'll support you all the way."

She shook her head. "No, thank you. I don't want to do anything of the sort. Thanks, Henry, for sorting that out and for the first aid kit."

"My pleasure. Is there anything else I can get you? We have a wonderful wedding brochure if you're thinking about making things official."

She grinned at him. "You heard that?"

He shook his head. "No, I just think that you two are one of those rare couples that are destined to be together whether they want to or not. Forgive me for speaking out of turn. I'm an old romantic at heart and sometimes people need a little push in the right direction. Not that I'm interfering in your business, because I'm not."

She laughed. "Is this a conspiracy. Did he ask you to say

that?"

"Not at all. I'm just saying what I see and what I see is two people who are in love who could do great things together. But enough of that, I'm off to make myself a pot of tea. Goodnight, both of you, and let me know if there are any further problems."

He nodded at them both and left them staring at each other. Maria laughed. "I like Henry."

Harrison nodded. "He's a good guy, I like him, too."

"Then make sure you tip him good, to make up for all the fuss I caused him."

He reached out for her hand. "Come on, let's get you back to bed. You have a busy day and need to rest while you can. I'll keep watch and make sure you have no more scary dreams."

They left the vodka and she let him lead her back up to the penthouse. She turned to look around the empty bar. Could she ever get used to living a life like this? Right now, she didn't know, but she was beginning to like the idea.

TWELVE

Frankie was already in the office when she arrived, a little blurry-eyed. He took one look at her. "You look like crap—did you not sleep?"

"No, I had a bad night. I feel like crap. Let's go get coffee. I need to eat."

Frankie was out of the office door before she'd even turned around. She didn't want to tell him she'd spent the night at the Plaza. And she definitely wasn't going to mention Harrison's offer to help her change career. Perhaps Frankie could work in the bookstore with her. He didn't read many books so wouldn't be a great asset, but it was comforting to know it was an option.

Sam's Deli was busy, but Marge gave them a wide grin as they walked in and pointed to the booth at the back that was free. It smelled so good—frying bacon and coffee. There was no smell like it when you were a little hungover. They squeezed in the booth and Frankie picked up a menu, despite the fact they'd ordered the same things every day for the last seven years.

"So, why do you feel like crap? Did Loverboy keep you up all night or could you not sleep because of the murders? Take it from me, alcohol isn't the answer. Did you know that whenever you drink your eyes go a little bloodshot the next morning?"

"Jeez, what are you, my mother?"

"Just stating the facts, Miller. So, what is it? Because the suspense is killing me?"

"Bad dreams about the Parker. And yes, I had a couple of glasses of vodka to help me get back to sleep."

"So, you didn't spend the night with Mr. Rich?"

Her head was pounding, and she needed coffee. "I did. He took me out for pizza and then we danced at his cousin's birthday party at the Plaza then ended up back in his suite. Is that enough detail or do you want more? Because if you do, it's gonna have to wait until I've eaten."

He smiled at her. "I'm impressed. You had a good night then?"

"Until I woke up screaming from the worst nightmare I've ever had, it was pretty good, yeah."

"Good, I'm glad. You should be out having fun."

Marge appeared with her notepad and pencil. Like Frankie, she pretended that she didn't know the score.

"You hungover this morning, sweetheart?"

Maria rolled her eyes. "Jeez, can I not do anything without the whole world knowing about it?"

Frankie winked at Marge. "Yes, she is. Take no notice of her, just feed her the usual and she'll come around. How are you doing, Marge?"

Maria put her elbows on the table and laid her head on them.

"Better than her, that's for sure."

Maria ignored her.

"Same as usual for you, Frankie?"

"Yes, please, Marge."

Marge scooped up the menus and sashayed to the counter to grab the coffee pot, returning to fill the two mugs. "Get this down you, Maria, and I'll bring you some Tylenol to go with your bagel. Don't say I'm not the best waitress in NYC. The Plaza might be all fancy, but they don't love you like I do."

Maria lifted her head and smiled at her. "Thank you, Marge, nobody is as good as you."

"Good, glad to hear it." She walked away with a huge grin on her face.

"We need to go back and check that room out, Frankie. I dreamed it was open. Someone had been inside it, and I think we better check it out to be sure. It really bothered me—and I think we missed something."

He nodded, ripping open little pots of creamer and adding some to both of their coffees. "We need to do that then, as soon as we've finished breakfast. What was your dream about?"

She shook her head then winced. "You definitely don't want to know; it was like I was being chased by Freddy Krueger on speed."

"Sounds fun."

"It wasn't."

He sipped the hot drink, staring out the window at the people hurrying past on their way to work, school or wherever they had to be. Maria wondered if she shouldn't have said anything to him about Harrison or her dream. Normally she'd have kept it quiet, but it must have been bothering her—a lot. How the hell did she get the wound on her shoulder? She found it hard to believe that a bed spring had suddenly popped up in the most expensive room in the Plaza. She should have asked Henry about that; why hadn't she? If she went back, she'd speak to him when Harrison wasn't around to find out the truth.

"What's our plan for today?"

She jerked and spilled coffee down the front of her black tee. Picking up a napkin, she blotted the stain.

"Gee, you're jumpy. That dream really got to you, huh?"

She nodded. "Plan is, we check out the room, see if we can

speak to the maintenance guys, and the contractors who go in and out. Somebody knew that room was out of use. It wasn't a guest or one of the long-term rentals. It had to be workers. And while we're at it, figure out where their feet could be."

"Addison said both sets of parents flew in last night after they were told the news by the Boston PD. They're probably going to want to speak to us at some point. Thought I'd better warn you about it."

She didn't need warning. If that were her child, God forbid, who had died so brutally and horrifically, she would want answers, too. "Then we better get a move on and find something to tell them."

Marge placed their breakfast orders on the table in front of them. "Terrible about those girls they found at the Parker."

"It is, Marge. It was horrific."

Reaching out a hand, Marge patted Maria's shoulder. Maria tried not to wince. When she had woken up again, it had been burning and painful to the touch. She was worried it was infected but didn't have the time to go get it checked out. There was too much to do.

"No wonder you needed a drink last night, sweetheart. I just don't know how you do it. How you can deal with the horrors that you have to every day."

Frankie took a bite out of his huge bagel, and spoke through a mouthful of mashed up bacon, eggs and cheese. "We do it because somebody has to, even though it damn well breaks our hearts."

"You are good people, and we appreciate you, we really do." Marge turned away but not before Maria noticed the tears pooling in the corner of her eyes. Frankie waited until Marge was out of hearing distance. "She's going soft in her old age."

Maria shushed him. "No, she's just got a heart tucked away inside that tough exterior. She's right though, Frankie. Some cases are worse than others. This one feels that way. Riley Holt, we found her and brought her home alive against all odds. There is no way we can do that for Dory and Michelle and that breaks my heart."

On the street outside the Parker Hotel, there was the normal hustle and bustle of city life. Life truly does go on, thought Maria, especially in New York City. Today some other horror would fill the news and the girls would be forgotten about. Most people probably already had forgotten.

As they approached the entrance, Maria tried to keep her eyes on the ground. She didn't want to see that blue smudge staring down at her from the tenth floor. The closer they got, the colder she felt, the chill going through her bones. But she wasn't going to let fear stop her from doing her job.

Inside there was no sign of Rick. She wondered if it was his day off. Instead, Shanice was at the reception desk, and she lifted a hand to greet them. Frankie headed straight for the elevators, where a handful of guests milled around. Maria couldn't help wondering if they'd been scared or saddened by the murders, or if they were just oblivious and determined not to let something so brutal spoil their vacation.

Inside the elevator, the trepidation inside Maria's gut worked extra fast to make her feel sick with fear. This place had gotten under her skin in more ways than one. She tried to stop the images of last night's nightmare from surfacing as they waited for the doors to open on the thirteenth floor.

As the doors slid apart, she could feel tiny, cold beads of fear breaking out all over her skin. If the lights went out like in the dream, that would be it—she was out of here. Thankfully, the hallway was bathed in light. In fact, it was far brighter than yesterday, and it looked like the bulbs had all been replaced with new ones. For a moment it occurred to her that maybe all the bulbs had blown last night. Had she been dreaming? Or was it a premonition?

Frankie pushed her forwards. Despite wanting to cling on to the elevator handrail, she found herself stepping out of it into the hallway. Her heart thumped so hard inside her chest that the noise filled her ears. The door still had the yellow crime scene tape crisscrossed over it, but it was clearly shut, and she felt her shoulders loosen a little.

"Damn it, we didn't get a key." Frankie strode towards the door. "You're gonna have to go back down and get one."

The cleaning cart was further down the hallway. Maria walked towards it, in the same direction that the shadow guy had come from last night. Although she didn't feel particularly brave, she wanted to see if there was anywhere for a person to hide. As she reached the corner, Rosa stepped out of a doorway and nodded at Maria.

"Morning, Rosa. Could you let us into room 1303 please?" Rosa crossed herself but nodded. "Thank you."

Maria carried on towards the end of the hallway where she found a small alcove with a large antique, ornate gilt mirror on the wall. Tucked next to it was a side table with an arrangement of silk flowers on top. Nowhere for a person to hide. Maria felt a little better. It had been a dream, an awful one that had scared her, but nevertheless, a dream.

Frankie ducked under the tape and entered the room before Maria reached him. He didn't yell or shout, so she figured it must be all as good as it could be in there. Maria ducked under, too, and looked at the empty, heavily bloodstained twin beds. Patches had been cut from the mattresses to be taken away for DNA testing. The room smelled of death and burning. The fire investigator had been thorough and fast, sending over a report which had been the first email she'd opened this morning. The curtains had gone up in seconds when the fire was started in a wastepaper bin underneath. This room needed more than a faulty faucet fixing now. The paintwork was blistered and peeling; it was a mess.

"Good morning. Shanice said you were here."

Rick stood with his arms crossed at the threshold to the room. He didn't try to come under the tape, nor cross it. Frankie pointed to the charred woodwork.

"It's a mess in here. Going to take some time to get this sorted."

"Talking of time frames, the directors are asking when we can have the room back so it can be sorted out."

"I'm going to be honest with you, Rick. That's not up to us, it's down to the fire department. So, you're gonna need to take it up with them. Our crime scene techs finished up late last night, so we don't need it."

Maria watched his face as he stared at the beds. There was no avoiding the deep, crimson stains that had bloomed like giant flowers all over the bottom part of each mattress where the girls' feet had been removed. Rickie's complexion looked a little paler and he whispered, "What do you suppose he did with the feet?"

Frankie shrugged. "Hard to say. Took them home and put them in the cooler so he can keep looking at them? Tossed them in the garbage? He could be walking around with them tucked into a backpack. We don't know that yet, and unless we catch him, I don't suppose we ever will."

Rick nodded, then walked away, but not without glancing back at Maria and catching her eye. It gave her the distinct impression he wanted to talk to her, just not in front of Frankie. She gave him a slight nod of her head. At some point, she was going to need to catch up with him. But right now, she wasn't sure she wanted to hear what he had to say.

THIRTEEN
1970

As it turned out, he didn't have to go very far to find a woman willing to go back to his hotel room. He'd decided to get a drink in the bar downstairs, to give himself a little Dutch courage before hitting the sidewalk. To his surprise, it was full of single women, and most were hookers. What kind of establishment let hookers use the bar so freely? That perturbed him until he'd realized it was to his advantage. As long as he kept it together and didn't act too stupid, he could have a good time here.

His gaze fell on a woman a little older than he'd like, but a quick glance told him she had tiny feet and wore a pair of red stilettos. That sealed the deal. So, he hit on her. Pretending he didn't know she was a hooker, he'd bought her drinks and used his charm until they were laughing and smiling as if they were old friends. She'd been pretty once, before working the streets stole her youth and beauty, but her eyes still sparkled in the dim lights when she laughed.

"Hey, you want to go somewhere where we can have a little privacy? We could continue this upstairs in my room."

He smiled at her, and she looked a little sad at his offer.

Then she shook her head. "I like you, you're funny and smart, but I can't do that, sorry."

Confused, he arched an eyebrow at her. "I thought we were having a good time?"

"We are, we have, and you have been the best company. But I'm not the kind of woman you think I am."

He stared down at those red shoes, those perfectly shaped feet tucked inside them, and felt the crotch of his jeans getting tight.

"Honey, I know exactly what kind of woman you are. The one who charges by the hour, and I don't care. I really like you and if it means I have to pay you to come up to my room where we can have a good time shooting the shit, then I will."

She stared into his eyes and for a moment he felt as though she was seeing right through to the darkest depths of his soul. But she picked up her wine glass, downed the rest of her drink, tucked her purse under her arm and smiled at him. "Come on, big spender, let's go empty your mini bar then."

She stood up and he quickly followed. His eyes darted around the room to see if anyone was paying attention. Nobody was—they were all too busy drinking, smoking and having a good time to be bothered with what he was doing. They got the elevator up to the thirteenth floor. He took hold of her hand and led her to his room. She looked around then smiled.

"I never made it this high up before. I know the alley out back real well and I've been in a couple of the staff rooms in the basement. I like you and I don't even know your name."

"I like you, too. It's Arnold but my friends call me Arnie." He paused because he didn't know hers either.

"Cherry."

He grinned at her, doubting that Cherry was her name, but that didn't matter because he wasn't called Arnie either, and he imagined she knew that, too. He did like her though; she was funny, and suddenly he didn't know if he could go through with what he'd planned. He should have gone to the bus station and found a girl there; someone he didn't want to spend time with, other than to remove her feet. He took two miniature bottles of whisky out of the bar and passed her one.

"Do you want ice?"

She shrugged. "Do you?"

He laughed, unscrewed the tiny cap and tipped the bottle into his mouth, feeling the warm liquid burn his throat. She giggled and uncapped her bottle. "I guess that's a no." She tipped her head back and did the same.

By the time they'd emptied the mini bar and eaten the snacks inside, he was just about ready to explode. She kicked off her shoes. It was hard to focus on her face when he could see the delicately painted red toenails that matched her shoes.

"You like my feet, huh? Have a thing for them?"

Shocked that she'd realized, he looked up at her. "They're pretty feet."

She lay on the bed; he sat next to her. Lifting her legs, she slowly moved her feet onto his lap, taking her time, letting them caress his thighs and lower back. He let out a low groan before he cupped hold of them, lowering his head to kiss them. He realized that she hadn't discussed how much this was going to cost him or asked for the money upfront. But he didn't care. All he could think about was how he was going to enjoy every single minute of Cherry whilst he could. He'd see how long he could control the insatiable ache deep inside him, before it got the better of him. Because, if and when it did, how much she planned to charge would be of no importance.

FOURTEEN

Maria had gained nothing from revisiting the room, so they headed back down to the reception area. As soon as they got out of the elevator, Frankie's phone rang and she saw a faint blush rise up his cheeks.

"I have to take this."

Then he walked towards the exit, leaving Maria wondering if it was a business call or from a woman. He rarely walked away from her to answer his phone. She knew more about his private life than she ought to, and it surprised her that he was keen to keep the call a secret. She headed towards the manager's office, where Shanice was playing a game on her phone with an expression of pure concentration.

"Hey, sorry to bother you. Is Rick around?"

The woman jolted, almost throwing her phone to the floor. "Gee, you were like a silent ninja. I didn't hear you approaching."

Maria grinned. "Thanks, I'll take that as a compliment."

"Rickie is in his office; said he wasn't to be disturbed, but I'll see if he's got a minute."

She began to type and as soon as she hit send the door to his office opened. He waved Maria to come around. She went inside and shut the door behind her.

"Where's your scary partner?"

"You think Frankie is scary?"

He nodded.

"He's outside. Did you want to talk to me?"

"Not really, but I couldn't sleep last night, so I'm going to tell you what I know. I keep my head down and ignore this stuff. It's easier for me to cope this way. I didn't believe anything like this was possible until I started working here, but it happens, and I feel bad for not warning you yesterday."

She didn't like the sound of where this was going. "Warning me?"

"The woman in blue. People say if you see her, it's a bad omen, that someone is going to die."

"You told me, didn't you?"

He shook his head. "I don't think so."

For a moment, Maria was puzzled, then she remembered it was one of those loud sisters who'd told her bad things happen when someone sights the blue woman. She'd taken it to mean bad things in general happened, not to a specific person.

"Are you saying I'm in danger?"

"I don't know. I just wanted to let you know to be extra careful, in case..." He didn't finish his sentence. She felt the stirrings of a cold chill kiss the skin across the back of her neck as she thought about the dream and the cut on her shoulder.

Rick stared at her. "Has something happened already?"

"I had a bad dream about this place last night, but after yesterday it's understandable. Just my cop brain trying to make sense of why someone would hurt those girls so bad."

"This place." He blew out a long, heavy breath through pursed lips and then continued, "It's okay on the outside and if you ignore the dark stuff bubbling underneath the surface, it's probably no different to any other hotel—if you're not stopping here very long. Once you scratch that surface and see what's underneath, though, it opens your eyes to things that most people would never realize can happen."

"Like what?" Maria tried to keep her voice calm, but he was freaking her out. She had an underlying sense that what he was telling her was the truth, as much as she wanted to discard every word and walk out of his office—an office that seemed to be closing in on her.

"Stanley, my predecessor, had this old blue leather notebook. It was kind of like an incident book for when things happened. Only this one was kept under lock and key in the safe and nobody but Stanley ever got to see it. He knew more about this place than I ever could, or would want to. I try to fill his shoes, but Stanley ran this place like clockwork. He knew what everyone needed and was probably the best hotel manager in the whole of New York. I only saw the blue book a couple of times, but it was thick. Full of handwritten notes from guests saying they had awful dreams where they were being chased through the corridors; newspaper articles about incidents that happened here or connected to the hotel. Over the years a handful of staff have seen the woman in blue up on the tenth. And... I don't know how to say this without scaring you to death."

"Tell me." Maria struggled to keep her voice neutral, even with terror building up inside her at the mention of guests being chased in their dreams.

"It didn't end well for them. Some died, one lost their foot in an elevator accident."

The chill was now like a full-on Arctic blast of sub-zero temperatures. Had she sealed her fate yesterday by picking out the blue smudge staring down at the street? And what was it with this place and feet?

"How did some of them die?"

Rickie's expression told her he wished he'd never brought

her in here. "We had one maid fall from the rooftop. Another maid had seen her running up the stairwell and called after her. The girl didn't answer and looked scared to death, as if she was being chased. Another had a cardiac arrest in room 1303. Rosa found her on the floor, eyes wide open, frozen, as if she'd been frightened so bad it caused her heart to stop. Her hands were clasped in the prayer position."

Maria regretted asking him how they'd died; she didn't want to hear any more. "Where's Stanley now. Is he still alive?"

"He lives in Brooklyn, or he did. He retired for good when the hotel had to close due to the Covid outbreak. He couldn't keep away even when they closed this place down in the early aughts—he kept coming back."

She peered over his shoulder at the huge safe behind the desk. "Did he leave the book behind?"

Rick shook his head. "I've never seen it since the day he left. To be honest, I don't ever want to."

"What about you? Do you keep a record of strange incidents like he did?"

"I keep a file on my computer. The hotel has been relatively ghost- and incident-free since Covid. I don't know if it's because nobody had the time to think about them or because Stanley retired and they left with him, but nobody has reported scary dreams or things coming out of the mirror and chasing them for a while."

"Until yesterday, that is. Maybe they were waiting for the right time to make an appearance? Why does Rosa think the devil lives in room 1303?"

"There was a murder inside that room back in the seventies. There have been a couple of suicides, too, as well as the maid found dead in there. But if you ask me, it's just an unlucky room. Although I don't rent it to anyone travelling solo just in case."

Her cell began to vibrate, and she saw Frankie's name. "I have to go, thanks for the warning, Rick."

"Take care."

She smiled but could not shake the feeling of uncertainty that hung over her, or the sense of impending doom. She needed to find Stanley and speak to him, but she wasn't sure if she wanted to do it alone—or with Frankie.

FIFTEEN

As she walked outside, the winter sunshine hit her face, warming her cheeks enough to make her feel a little better. Frankie leaned against a wall, sipping a coffee from a cardboard cup. He passed the other coffee to her. "Where the hell have you been? I was gonna send a search party in."

"Thanks for the coffee, and sorry. I wanted a quick chat with your friend Rick."

"About?"

"The whole vibe of this hotel. It's off—can't you feel it?"

One of his thick, bushy eyebrows arched at her and she shrugged. "What are you, some kind of expert now on creepy shit?" he said.

"No, but something is going down in there. Do you not feel it whenever you go inside? Frankie, we've both been through some stuff, so I think we know when something is off."

"I get that it's creepy and some weird stuff is happening, but why don't we concentrate on the investigation and not go back *there* unless we absolutely have to?"

Maria was stunned by his change of heart from the last investigation. If he wanted to ignore anything that could be supernatural, perhaps their time in Beacon Hill had gotten to him more than she realized.

"Yeah, okay. Let's go view the footage Rick sent over and see if we can spot the girls going into the hotel and see who they're with."

He clamped his hand on her shoulder, making her wince. He didn't notice her pain and she wasn't about to tell him. She headed back in the direction of the car, wondering if she should have got some antiseptic ointment to put on the deep wound. She'd stop off at the Duane Reade near the precinct and get some just in case. She'd rather take precautions than let it become a mess.

Sipping her cappuccino, Maria pushed all thoughts of that dream and the Parker from her mind. Enough was enough. They had a killer to catch, and she was turning into a real softie. She didn't like it.

Three hours of footage later, Maria let out a yell so loud Frankie knocked over the open can of Pepsi on his desk.

"Jeez, are you trying to kill me?" he growled while frantically moving folders before the brown, fizzy liquid soaked through them.

"I have them walking in but they're not with anyone. At least, I don't see anyone close by."

Frankie's chair scraped against the floor as he came around to look at her screen. There they were, in full view, as clear as day. Two girls with backpacks strolling into the hotel as if they were guests; as if they had been there before. They didn't falter. They headed straight towards the two elevators at the far end and pushed the call button. The doors opened, and the girls disappeared from sight as the glass slid shut.

"Had they been in the Parker before? They look so confident, as if they're supposed to be there. We need to ask their parents. What time are they due into town?"

He flicked his wrist to look at his watch. "Maybe another hour, two hours. As soon as they land, the family liaison officer is going to pick them up and bring them to the morgue. We could speak to them there."

"Frankie, I don't think they're going to want a barrage of questions after seeing their dead daughters. Who's liaising? I'll ask them to talk to them about the Parker and see if they have visited before."

The phone on Maria's desk pierced the air with a shrill ring and she grabbed it quick. The loud sound was enough to give her anxiety. "Miller."

"Is Conroy with you?"

Addison sounded even more stressed than usual. "Yes, sir, he is."

"Good, I have two sets of very emotional parents in the family room. Do you have anything of substance we can give them, to make it look as if we're moving fast on this?"

Maria felt her stomach clench at the thought of having nothing whatsoever to give them. "I'm afraid we don't have much, except some CCTV footage of the girls going into the hotel."

"Christ, Miller, I needed more than that. You better come speak to them yourselves. Tell Conroy I said so in case he tries to get out of it."

He slammed the receiver down, leaving her with a dial tone. Frankie didn't need telling who she'd been speaking to. "He's going to give himself a coronary one day. It's unnecessary, the stress he causes himself and everyone else around him. What's up now?"

"Parents are already here, in the family room downstairs, waiting for us."

"They are, huh? What is it you always say to me? Be careful

what you wish for. Maybe I'll wish for the Powerball numbers to come up this week."

"Do you do the Powerball?" He shook his head. "Well, you're kind of at a disadvantage then, aren't you?"

"I guess I am. Then I'll put a line on, Ms. Smarty Pants, and we'll see if it works. Those numbers come up and I'm buying myself a beach house down in the Florida Keys. No more dead bodies or scary monsters for this guy. I'll retire and live the dream; I'll buy you one, too, so you can still see my handsome face each day for breakfast. We can live right next to each other."

Maria smiled, wishing that one day he would get to retire somewhere beautiful and enjoy his life stress-free. He was ten years older than her and getting nearer to retirement. She would miss him like crazy when that time came. Maybe she'd leave policing when he did and see if Harrison would help her sort out that bookshop/café idea. "Gee, thanks. You're too kind. I don't know if I want to see your face every day for the rest of my life, though."

He laughed. "Bull crap, you know you couldn't live without me."

They took the stairs down to the family room. Maria had a thin cardboard file tucked under her arm with hastily printed stills of the girls walking into the Parker. Arriving on the landing, they found Addison pacing, looking as if he'd rather be anywhere than here. She felt the same way; grieving parents were hard to deal with. It hurt deep down inside her heart, the pain they were going through.

Addison and Frankie hung back, and Maria sighed. Both of them were babies when it came to dealing with grief-stricken relatives. Maria rapped gently on the door twice before opening it. The two men standing inside turned to look at her. Their eyes were wide and eyebrows raised high. Maria knew instantly that they were both in shock, still trying to come to terms with the life-changing, dreadful news that had been passed to them about their daughters yesterday. The two moms sat on chairs, eyes red and puffy, tissues in hand. Both looked exhausted and Maria wished she could rewind time, go back to when the girls got off the bus. She'd pick them up and keep them safe from harm. How many grieving parents, spouses, partners, siblings, would give anything for that chance? Everyone stared at her, and Frankie arrived at her side, which jolted her into action.

"Mr. and Mrs. Painter, Mr. and Mrs. Carter, I'm so sorry for your loss, and that you are here under the most dreadful of circumstances."

The men gave a curt nod, in sync with each other. The women sobbed and Maria felt horrible. No matter what she did or said, it wasn't going to change the fact that Dory and Michelle were dead. It wasn't going to bring them home alive. She wanted to let them know that she was grieving their loss, too, but it wasn't what they wanted, and she knew that. They wanted answers and right now that was all she could try to give them.

"I'm afraid it's very early in the investigation and we haven't got a lot to go on at the moment. Would you take a look at these stills and see if it's your daughters in them for me? We need to identify how they got to the Parker Hotel and if they'd been there before."

Michelle's parents looked shocked. Dory's glanced at each other briefly, not so surprised at the mention of the hotel. Maria passed two sets of stills to them.

Mr. Painter muttered, "That goddamn hotel."

Maria gave them a few more seconds with the photographs. Mrs. Carter nodded and cried at the same time. Mr. Carter reached out and put his hands on his wife's shoulders, and said, "Yes, that's Dory and Michelle. But I don't understand what they were doing there in the first place. As far as we knew, they were having a sleepover at Dory's house."

Mrs. Painter stared her straight in the eye. "And Dory asked permission to have a sleepover at Michelle's. Neither of them mentioned getting on a bus and coming into New York, because that would have been a definite no."

Frankie nodded. "Mr. Painter, what did you mean when you said that goddamn hotel?"

"Dory has—had—an obsession with it. This isn't the first time she's been there without adult supervision."

Both Michelle's parents turned to stare at him, horror etched across their faces. Maria knew that their shock was going to turn to anger rapidly and asked, "Why, why was she obsessed with it?"

"She read some book about haunted hotels last year after we stayed at the Parker for a two-night Christmas shopping trip. She kept saying she thought it was creepy and after we came home, she started to have nightmares. So, she read more books she ordered off Amazon. Ever since then she has talked about nothing else. She snuck out of the house a couple of months ago and came here, on her own. She tried to talk to the staff about ghosts, but she said they weren't very helpful. Took lots of pictures then got the bus back before we even realized she was out of town."

There was a look of pure horror on Mrs. Carter's face. "This is Dory's fault. She got them killed. It's your fault for letting her go there. What kind of parents are you? Letting your kid get the bus to go looking around a hotel she had no business visiting?"

Mr. Painter bowed his head. "If I'd known they were coming here I would have stopped them. I didn't know."

Mrs. Painter's sobs were getting louder, higher, and she was on the verge of losing it completely. Maria knew she had to do something.

"Teenagers are stubborn and very adept at getting what they want, no matter what. This isn't anyone's fault except the guy who killed them. There is little point trying to blame each other. All that is going to do is make you bitter and resent each other. We need to work together to get the answers we need to find him."

Mrs. Carter stood up. She turned to her husband and hissed, "We're leaving, I can't do this. I don't want to be here in the same room as them. This is all their fault." She stormed to the door, almost sending Maria flying backwards as she pushed past her. Her husband followed. Turning as he left, he said, "We'll meet you at the mortuary. It might be best if we go first on our own until my wife calms down."

And then they were gone. Christina, the family liaison officer, rushed after them, followed by Addison. Mr. Painter took a seat beside his wife. His ashen face gave Maria cause for concern; he looked ill.

"This is hard. Everyone reacts differently. Mr. Painter, are you okay? Sir, do you need a medic?"

He shook his head. His wife glanced at his face and frowned. "David, did you take your tablets this morning?" Then she looked at Maria. "He has a heart condition."

Frankie turned to grab the phone off the wall. He dialed 911 and asked for paramedics to attend.

"I forgot to pack them. I'm okay." He looked at Frankie. "Really, I'll be okay—it's just the shock of it all."

Frankie knelt on the floor beside him. "Sir, we need to get you checked out, okay? If we don't then we are sadly lacking. We have a duty of care towards you both and I can't let you walk out of here if you're a ticking time bomb. Let the paramedics come check you out and get you some meds."

He nodded and reached for his wife's hand. She clasped his fingers tight, but she was staring at Maria.

"This is our fault. We knew Dory and Michelle both talked a lot about going to the hotel but they never, not once, said they were going to go on their own. I asked Dory to promise me she would wait until one of us could take her, and she agreed."

"You mentioned she had nightmares about the hotel. Did she ever tell you what they were?"

Frankie arched an eyebrow in her direction, but she ignored him. There was a deep feeling of unease making her stomach churn. She had to know.

"She didn't really talk about her nightmares much. She said they were too scary, but she did mention being chased after the first one. She always had a very vivid imagination and had night terrors as a child. She disliked mirrors and I remember her telling me about a haunted mirror or mirrors in the hotel. I dismissed them, and her dreams, as if they were nothing more than a child's vivid imagination. I should have listened to her more. I'm never going to get that chance now." Mrs. Painter crumpled then, at the thought of her little girl alive and safe, back when she could control her actions and keep her safe.

"I'm sorry, Mrs. Painter, I really am, to keep asking questions, but did Dory ever mention anyone specific at the hotel? Was there anyone who she spoke with, had got to know?"

"Not that I'm aware of. The only person she mentioned was some manager called Stanley who she said had retired. He was in the book she read."

There was a gentle knock on the door and Christina walked in followed by two paramedics. She smiled at Maria. "I'll take it from here, if you're good. As soon as we've got Mr. Painter checked out, I'm meeting the Carters at the morgue. Mr. Painter, we'll get you to the hotel and let you rest up a little before we do the next part, is that okay?"

He nodded. Maria wished she could do more. She lifted her hand to swipe at her brow; she was too warm, cooped up in this room with the Painter's. Their grief was making her feel unwell. "I'm sorry for your loss, we both are." She walked out of the door, paused then asked, "Did Dory ever mention seeing the woman in blue at the hotel?"

Mr. Painter shook his head, but Mrs. Painter nodded. "She said something about seeing a blue lady the first night we stayed there. But I didn't take much notice. I don't believe in ghosts or anything supernatural and I told her the same. That it's a pile of crap, made up by the same people who cash in on all the other holidays we have. I mean, Valentine's Day and Easter are all just excuses to get everyone to spend their hard-earned money on cards and chocolate we don't need."

Maria felt bile rise up her throat and knew she was going to vomit. She rushed past Frankie towards the toilets down the corridor, slamming the door open so hard the entire building shook. She reached the cubicle just in time, as she emptied the contents of her stomach into the bowl. Her hands clutched her knees as she bent double and retched until there was nothing left to come out. Her hands and her legs felt as if they didn't belong to her and she felt too warm, too hot and clammy. Pushing herself up, she leaned her forehead against the cool metal of the door and wished she'd never set foot in that hotel. Why had she picked up the phone? There was so much going on inside her head and she felt shaky, too hot, and her shoulder was burning.

"Hello, are you okay in there?"

She'd no idea who'd just asked her that. "Yeah, I'm good." She slid the catch across and opened the door.

The female paramedic stood there. "Your partner asked me to come and see if you were okay. Tough job, huh?"

She nodded. "Actually, I hurt my shoulder last night. Could you take a look at it for me? It's painful and feels as if it's burning."

"Sure thing, slip your shirt off."

It took Maria a couple of attempts because her fingers were trembling so much, but she did as she'd been told. She shrugged the shirt down, and the paramedic let out a small gasp. "Ma'am, that's a real mess and infected. You need stitches, too."

Maria looked in the mirror and saw that the dressing was soaked in blood. It was weeping yellow pus as well. "We need to get that cleaned and stitched up or you're going to get sepsis, if you haven't already. How do you feel?"

"Clammy, sick, shaky."

"Well, the good news is the guy with the bad heart is okay. He just needs his medication and rest. Under the circumstances, it's no wonder he's looking so ill. The bad news is if you don't let us take you to the hospital and get that wound cleaned out, you're going to end up seriously ill, if not dead."

She removed the dressing that Harrison had put over the cut last night, cleaned around it with some liquid that made Maria wince and taped a fresh dressing on top of it. Then she helped Maria put her shirt back on, fastening the buttons for her. "Come on, we'll get you fast-tracked, no waiting around, I promise."

Maria smiled. "Thank you, I'd appreciate that. I'm kinda up to my neck in it."

She nodded. "I know, I saw the news story last night and recognized you as the officer coming out of the hotel. It's horrific —those poor girls."

"It is. I need to find out what happened to them before it happens again."

"You do and thank God that we have good detectives like you. But if we don't get your shoulder sorted, you won't be in any state to do anything."

Maria smiled. "No waiting?"

"Nope, I'll make sure you get seen ASAP."

"Thank you. I'd better tell Frankie."

They went outside where Frankie was leaning against the wall, a look of concern on his face.

"Jeez, you look like crap."

"I feel it."

The paramedic smiled at him. "Maria needs to come with us and get her shoulder cleaned up. She won't be long and will phone you when she's been sorted."

"What... she's going with you, willingly? Must be bad." He reached out and gently placed the back of his hand on her forehead. "You have a temperature. Ring me when you're done, unless you want me to come with you?"

"No, don't waste time. Can you try to find out an address for Stanley? We need to go and talk to him as soon as possible."

"I'm on it." He looked at the paramedic. "Take care of her, otherwise I'll have to do all the work."

"I will."

Then he turned and walked away, leaving Maria to be escorted out of the building. For once she didn't care who might see her looking this way because she knew she was sick. But she worried that no amount of antibiotics could cure her. She'd seen the woman in blue with her own eyes and was scared it meant she was going to die, just like the girls on the thirteenth floor.

SIXTEEN

Maria drifted in and out of consciousness. The bright lights hurt her eyes. She could hear the beeps of the machines around her and the voices in the ER, but she couldn't stay focused. Maria was exhausted and so hot, yet at the same time her entire body shook like she was frozen to the core. She hadn't argued as they'd led her into a small side room and set up an IV. Maria hadn't even asked what was in it as she lay on her side while the doctor examined her shoulder. "How did you do this again, Maria?"

"I was in bed having a nightmare. I must have been thrashing around and caught it on a loose spring."

There was a long pause and she felt herself drifting away again, until the doctor's voice brought her back. "It looks like a knife wound. Are you sure you weren't stabbed? This is a safe place, and we can get you help if you need it."

She laughed, then stopped because it hurt her head and shoulder too much. "Thanks, I appreciate it. It was definitely a dream; I woke up with the pain in my shoulder."

"Well, it's infected and deep, so you better get yourself a new mattress."

Maria squeezed her eyes shut; the local anesthetic was working but the feel of the suture needle piercing her skin made her feel queasy. She drifted off—and found herself back in the Parker.

It was dark outside the windows and the hallway lights were dimmed. The elevator doors opened on the thirteenth floor. Maria let out a low moan. She didn't want to be here; she was too ill to fight whatever dark thing was stalking these halls. She jabbed her finger on the ground floor button repeatedly. Nothing happened. She walked out into the hallway and the doors shut behind her with a loud ping. The ancient lift began its journey down to the tenth floor, according to the display.

Maria looked for the stairs. She wasn't going anywhere near room 1303. Low whispers filled the air from every direction, but she ignored them. Seeing the emergency exit sign for the stairs, she walked towards them. It felt as if she was wading through molasses; she could barely lift her feet off the carpet. When she looked down, she let out a silent scream, stuffing her fist into her mouth to stop the sound. They were covered in a thick, black, glutinous, liquid that she felt sure was congealing blood. The entire carpet was covered in a layer of it—and then the smell hit her. So strong and intense, she retched as she lifted her arm to cover her nose. It was as if a hundred people had been slaughtered and left to bleed out up here.

She had to reach those stairs, had to get out before the monster knew she was back. A high-pitched scream filled the air, closely followed by another. Maria looked over her shoulder to see the two dead girls staring at her from the open doorway of room 1303. Their eyes were cloudy and white, and they had deep red grooves around their necks. The horrific part was they were standing on the stumps of their legs where their feet should have been, a river of blood flowing from them, making it impossible for Maria to walk.

"Help us, Maria, help us." They spoke without opening their mouths.

Maria shook her head. She couldn't move. She blinked, hoping to wake herself up. But when she opened her eyes, they were standing directly in front of her, so close she could see maggots wriggling underneath the soft tissue of their eyes and could smell the decomposition of their rotting corpses. She was going to throw up all over herself.

"Help us, Maria. He won't let us go. He's coming... he's coming back and this time he wants you."

Dory Painter reached out a dead, cold finger and prodded her in the chest, then she leaned closer—the smell was unbearable—and screamed, "He's coming!"

Maria jolted in the hospital bed. Her eyes flew open in fear, her heart racing. She tried to sit up and saw a familiar face sitting on the chair next to her bed, holding a book. She lifted a hand to reach out and touch him, to see if he was there or if she was hallucinating.

"Hey, were you having another bad dream? You were thrashing around. I was about to call the nurse to come and see if you needed something. How are you doing, Maria?"

Her mouth felt dry, but she didn't feel as hot or shaky as she had earlier. She pushed herself up. "What are you doing here?" She glanced out of the window and saw darkness when it should still have been daylight. She wasn't about to tell him she'd had another nightmare. He might insist she see a shrink.

"Frankie called—he was worried about you. I said I'd come to see you. You must have needed that sleep."

Her cheeks were already flushed pink from the temperature, but she could feel them getting hotter.

"I'm okay. I feel much better. Why the hell did he bother you? I'm sorry, Harrison, you can go now. I'm fine."

He scooted the chair towards the bed and took hold of her hand. "What, you're just going to send me home? I want to be

with you and make sure you're okay. The doc said if you
responded to the IV antibiotics, he would see if you could come
home, as long as there is somebody there to take care of you."

Maria pushed herself up. "I have to get out of here. There's
too much to do and I've wasted far too much time already."

"I told them I'd take responsibility for you and take you
back to my place. It's not a choice, Maria. If you want to leave,
then you have to come back with me. You can choose where
you'd rather stay, the Plaza or my place."

She didn't want to go back to the Plaza. "Your place."

He smiled. "That's good. I'll go get the doc and see if we can
get you signed out. You're not allowed to go to work for another
twenty-four hours at least."

She felt a rising tide of anger at him trying to tell her what
to do. "Before you get worked up, I had Frankie drop some files
off for you and your laptop. He said there's not much happened
since you came in here. He has the address of some guy you
need to speak to, but he can't see you both until tomorrow."

Frustrated and exhausted, she sank back onto the hard
pillows on the hospital gurney. "Thanks, I appreciate that."

"I'll go see if I can get you discharged." He left her staring
after him. She had no idea why she was so mad at him when
he'd given up his time to come and sit with her.

A nurse came in. "Time to check your dressing, honey, and
take your observations. If they're back in the normal range you
are good to go, with some antibiotics to take home with you."

"Thanks. Do you know how long that guy has been sitting
in here?"

She frowned at Maria. "Don't tell me you don't know him?
He's been here a couple of hours, sweetie."

"He's my good friend. I just didn't expect to see him."

"Well, he came in here demanding to speak to the doctor
and is the reason you can go home if your temperature is down.
You're supposed to be in here on twenty-four-hour watch, but

he promised he'd take good care of you and hire a private nurse if needed." She lowered her voice. "He gave his address as the Towers at the Waldorf. Girl, if some guy was going to whisk me away to his luxury penthouse and take care of me... unless he was a psycho, I'd be out of here in seconds, if you get my drift." She winked at Maria who smiled back.

"Yeah, he's a good guy. Too good for me." She let out a sigh and the nurse dead-eyed her.

"Who told you that? Nobody is too good for anybody. If you get along with each other and have the same sense of humor—which if you ask me is the most important thing in the world—and if you want a relationship to last, then it doesn't matter where anyone comes from. Don't you go believing that he's too good for you. Maybe you're too good for him—did you ever stop to think about that?"

"Cassie, what in the world are you doing in there? You know there's no time for you to go round giving out your relationship advice."

An older woman stood at the door with her hands crossed, staring at the younger nurse who was writing down Maria's temperature and waiting for the blood pressure cuff to go tight. "Sorry, Sister Angela."

Sister Angela nodded, then turned to Maria. "I hate to say this but she's right most of the time. So whatever advice she gave you, I'd take it." She turned to Cassie. "Now, back to work: how is the patient doing? Are we happy for her to leave?"

Cassie turned to her. "Yes, everything is back in the normal range."

Harrison, who had been standing behind the sister, smiled at all three of them. "Ladies, the doctor agrees I'm good to take Ms. Miller home."

Cassie turned to Maria and winked, making her laugh out loud. "I'll go get your tablets, won't be long."

Harrison sat on the edge of Maria's bed. "Are you okay with

this? If you'd rather go to your apartment, then I'll come with you instead."

She reached out and stroked his cheek. "No, I think it would be quite nice to be pampered a little. I guess it's time to check out your place."

His grin stretched across his whole face, making him look younger than his forty years.

"Where is Frankie?" she asked then.

"He's got a hot date apparently."

Her mouth dropped open. She felt a surge of jealousy, despite her lover sitting opposite her. Truth be told, she had a thing for Frankie deep inside that she was scared to acknowledge or do anything about. She tried to keep her voice neutral. "He has? Who with?"

"He called her the doc. Means nothing to me. He said not to tell you if I thought it might upset you."

Maria forced herself to smile. "The sly old dog. He must have asked out Betsy Conner, the medical examiner. He was flirting with her yesterday at the crime scene."

"Are you upset?"

She laughed, praying it didn't sound as false as it felt. "No, I'm overjoyed. He deserves a little fun and happiness. He's had a tough time. In fact, if anything, I guess I feel relieved that he's moving on."

She knew she should be relieved that Frankie was no longer moping around after her or Christy. It meant she could freely enjoy the time she spent with Harrison, instead of always worrying in the back of her mind about how Frankie was feeling. It was for the best—but in that moment it didn't feel that way.

SEVENTEEN

This time it was a little more complicated. The tenth floor was residential and those two sisters who lived up there were more observant and into everybody else's business than they had a right to be. Nobody expected it to happen again. He'd learned his lesson. There wouldn't be another failed attempt at setting the room on fire. It had announced what he'd done in a more spectacular way than a full-page advertisement in the *New York Times*. Instead, he'd leave her body there until the maids came in—and they would come in. That was part of the appeal of living in the Parker. The maids were shit hot. Stanley had trained them well and Rickie was a half-decent replacement, though he could never fill his boots.

The tenth floor was creepy, while the thirteenth was the stuff nightmares were made of. He liked the tenth best, because from there he could get direct access to the roof and the water tower, which was where he spent most of his time when working. Not always consciously, either. Sometimes he'd wake up there in a daze. He wondered if whatever lurked in the hotel helped itself to his body and made him do the terrible things he'd done. He'd read stories of normal people who'd kill and blame it on being possessed. He wasn't sure that was a real possibility, but it would explain a lot of what was happening to him. He had blackouts that lasted for a couple of hours, and the voice that talked to him when he was on his own quite frankly terrified him.

Looking down at the body on the bed, he wondered why there was so much blood. Then he saw the amputated foot and almost puked, but managed to stop himself. Could they get DNA from vomit? Probably.

The woman had been a little weird. She'd kept to herself, not mixed with anyone else. If she hadn't worn those black, shiny heels he would never have taken any notice of her. She didn't stand out in any other way. He had been working, replacing the socket in the hallway, when she walked past him. He'd seen her feet before he saw her. When she strolled past in those shoes, it was as if time stood still. He'd no idea why she had such a profound effect on him, but she had, and now look at this mess.

The metallic tang of pooling blood turned his stomach. The foot left splotches of blood all over the carpet as he walked to the kitchen area to find something to wrap it in. He used a roll of paper towels to wrap the foot as if he was applying a crepe bandage. Then he looked for something he could hide it in and found a plastic bag. It only needed to last long enough to get the foot up to the water tower. He wouldn't risk taking it home with him this time. The journey to and from work was too far; there were too many chances of some dog sniffing it out.

Oblivious to the mess he'd made, or the fact that a police search dog would sniff out the route he'd taken, he walked out of the apartment, trying to look as if he was supposed to be there. Nobody was around. Lately, the hallways were deserted, which was a good thing for him. About to crack open the door to the roof, he saw movement behind him. From the corner of his eye, he saw a flash of blue. By the time he'd turned around, it had gone. It left him feeling a little perturbed—had he just seen the woman in blue? He knew what that meant: something bad was going to happen to him or someone he knew. Maybe it had already happened. The thought of dying terrified him; the thought of making someone else die didn't. He knew deep down that this was a screwed-up way of thinking, yet he didn't care. Had no empathy with his victims. He only cared about himself. This, he thought, was exactly why he was in this situation.

He dashed up the stairs, taking them two at a time. Bursting onto the roof, he almost dropped the foot onto the floor. Standing in front of him was the woman who'd started all the fuss the other day when she'd discovered the fire.

"Oh, hey. You made me jump. Nobody comes up here. The roof is off limits to guests. Did you not see the sign on the door?"

She looked him up and down. Her eyes paused on the plastic bag he was clutching for a little longer than he'd have liked, as she exhaled a cloud of cigarette smoke. "Why are you up here then?"

"Lunch. I come up here to eat when it gets a bit too busy in there."

She smiled. "And that is exactly what I'm doing. When I find it all a little too much, I like to come up here and pace around, have a smoke in peace, even though I know they're bad for me. It's probably the cleanest air I can get without having to travel miles on the subway. I hate traveling that way."

He nodded. "Yeah. Look, I won't say anything about you coming up here to Rickie if you don't tell him I come up here for lunch, because I probably shouldn't be doing that either, you know."

She grinned. "Deal. What you got, anything exciting? I'm pretty hungry and could do with some inspo."

He felt rising panic at the thought of her looking inside the bag. His mouth was dry, and he wondered if the words would come out. "Nah, just pastrami on rye."

She pulled a face. "Yuck, you can keep that then. See you around." She bent her head to read his name tag, but he'd purposely turned it back to front. She took hold of it, and he got a whiff of the perfume she was wearing. It was pretty. She smelled a little like a walk on a tropical beach. "Arnie," she said to herself.

She waved, flicking the cigarette butt over the edge of the rooftop to land on some unsuspecting New Yorker's head below.

"Enjoy your pastrami, Arnie."

The door slammed shut behind her, just as a big, red splotch of blood hit the rooftop. He felt as if his heart was going to explode inside his chest. He ran to the water tower and left the foot on a high ledge with the other two. They were looking a little the worse for wear now, mottled green and black. He was thankful it was cold and not a stinking hot summer's day, or the smell would have been unbearable. He was also glad there were no flies around this time of year; otherwise, the place would have been crawling with blow flies and maggots.

EIGHTEEN

Maria woke up drenched in sweat. She was alone in a bed the size of her entire bedroom and she was out of breath. This time she had no recollection of her nightmare, and for that small mercy she was grateful. But she knew it involved the Parker. For that reason alone, she didn't probe too deeply to remind herself what she'd been doing in that God-awful hotel.

Picking her phone off the charging pad, she almost had a coronary when she saw that it was noon. She threw back the covers and scrambled out of bed. Maria felt a lot better than she had yesterday, but still not like her normal self. There was a knock on the door and for a moment she panicked. Harrison would be at work, so who was knocking? "Hello?"

"Good morning, ma'am. Mr. Williams said to leave you undisturbed but when you woke up to see if there is anything I can get for you."

Maria opened the door to see a pretty Hispanic woman wearing jeans and a black roll-neck jumper. She could have passed as her double, except for being a little older than her.

"Good morning. I'm sorry, I don't know your name."

"Estha. I'm his housekeeper, although sometimes I feel like his mother." She rolled her eyes, making Maria laugh.

"Well, Estha, I'm good. I need to shower and get to work. I'm way too late."

"Oh, you don't have to worry about that. Mr. Williams brought your work to you." She beamed, and Maria heard a familiar, gravelly voice call out to her from the lounge.

"Jeez, I thought you died in there, Miller. What time do you call this?"

Maria stared at Estha. "Am I dreaming still?"

Estha shook her head. "No, your partner has set up a mobile office on the dining table, at Mr. Harrison's request. He also said to tell you he left you a note under your pillow and that he hopes you don't work too hard. He's going to be checking in on you... in a non-stalker kind of way."

Maria laughed. "He did, huh? If he phones, you tell him I said thank you and I'm good."

"I'll let you get a shower then make you brunch. Is there anything you would like?"

"Coffee and bagels are always good for me."

Estha smiled. "Ah, an easy guest. You need to stop over more often."

She turned and left Maria staring down the hallway, tempted to pinch herself in case she was dreaming. There were Sak's and Chanel bags on the floor next to a closet with a note taped to the door that read 'Maria'. She opened the door and gasped. Suits, jeans, roll-neck jumpers and assorted tees, along with several pairs of new Nikes and some black Dr Marten boots. Surely, they weren't for her? Retrieving the note from under her pillow, she opened the heavy, cream envelope to take out the single sheet of paper.

Good morning, beautiful. You scared me yesterday. I hope you're feeling much better. Please don't be mad that I got Estha to go out and get you some new clothes, shoes and boots. I wasn't sure how long I would have you to myself and didn't want you worrying about changing your clothes. I know you don't like fussy. If you've met Estha, you will see that she has very similar taste in clothes to you. I think you'll like what she's chosen. Take what you need and please don't work too hard. You still need to rest up. If you're still here later, we'll eat in. Estha is a wonderful cook. Tell her what you would like and leave the rest up to her. I think Frankie should be here by now. Use whatever you need. See you later, H xx

Tears pricked at the corner of her eyes. Even though she wanted to be annoyed with Harrison, she couldn't. This was his way of taking care of her. She grabbed what she needed, laying the clothes on the bed. There was even a drawer full of new underwear, all very practical and very much her style. Slipping off the straps of the slip she'd gone to bed in, she looked at her shoulder. The skin around the waterproof dressing was no longer a burning, hot mess. It was still pink, swollen and painful but to her relief, it was nowhere near as bad as it had been yesterday.

When she joined Frankie, he was sipping a coffee and eating a bagel. He looked up at her and smiled.

"Boy, do you look better than you did yesterday. I thought you were gonna die at one point." He swiped his fingers across his neck in a chopping action.

"Thanks, that's kind of you to say. I feel better, or at least better than I did."

"You did okay with this guy, you know that, right? I'm amazed he still has a thing for you, considering the number of times you brushed him off. But he does and it's cool that he does."

She pulled out a chair opposite, sat down and picked up a hot, buttered bagel. "It is?"

"Oh yeah, we could all do with a super-rich guy in our lives, including me. This way I get to experience what it's like to live this way without having to do anything in return. It's a win-win situation for me. So, if you don't mind a little advice from your uncle Frankie, enjoy it while you can and stop being so hard on the guy."

Maria arched one eyebrow. "Who are you, my mom? And where did you get to last night when I was in my hour of need? What if I hadn't wanted Harrison to come to my rescue?" Frankie's mouth dropped open. "You had a date with the doctor, I heard. I'll forgive you because you need a little happiness in your life, too. Which doc?"

His cheeks went a deep shade of crimson. "Doctor Conner —Betsy. I'm sorry, Maria. I had no idea you needed me. I would never have—"

She held up a hand. "Stop, I'm not being serious. I'm glad you had a date." Despite her initial pangs of jealousy, hearing about the date from Frankie, seeing his excitement, she found that she was glad. "How did it go?"

"We're seeing each other Saturday."

A whoop of delight left Maria's lips and she clapped her hands together. "Good. Now that the pair of us might actually be having a social life outside of work, where are we at? Harrison said you'd tracked down Stanley. Have you talked to him?"

"No, I thought I'd wait for you. Here's what we have so far. I printed off the list of employees who have access to the rooms. There are twelve. Out of the twelve, I narrowed it down to seven guys, because I've got to be honest with you, Maria, I don't see a woman doing this kind of thing."

He passed a sheet of paper to her, and she read through the names. None were familiar. "You've run them through the system?"

"Not yet—I'm not Superman. I had to go home, eat and sleep in between babysitting you and my date."

She smiled. "Did you bring a laptop?"

He picked a bag off the floor and put it on the table, sliding it towards her. "Be my guest. You might be a bit incapacitated, but you're not dead."

"You're such an asshole."

He shrugged, lifting the coffee cup to his lips to hide the smile threatening to break out.

"Stanley lives in a nice apartment block overlooking Coney Island Beach. I've told him we'll be paying him a visit in the next couple of hours and he's waiting for us."

Maria was grateful that Frankie had been busy while she was out of action. He was a good cop, always had been. "Thank you."

"For what? Doing my job. You know, I was thinking we should get Harrison to ask one of his team to do some digging in the news archives about the hotel, the killer that stalked the halls back in the seventies and whatever else they can find. It would save us a lot of time; he has the resources. It would be frivolous of us not to abuse them."

Maria agreed. Why not use what help Harrison could give them? "I'll ask him. How did the morgue visit go? Are the parents still here or did they fly home?"

"Michelle's parents flew home straight after; Dory's are still here; they said they felt closer that way. They booked themselves a room in the Parker."

"You're kidding me?"

"Straight up. Kind of get that they'd want to feel close to Dory, but not sure I'd want a room in the hotel she was murdered in. It's concerning if you ask me. I'm worried her pops is going to take the matter in his own hands."

"We better get a move on then." She looked at the list he'd given her minutes ago. Dates of birth were next to each name.

Two guys were in their sixties, two in their fifties. A thirty-eight-year-old and two in their late twenties. "Hard to call it."

He nodded. "I'm going for one of the fifty-year-olds."

"I think it's the guy who's thirty-eight. He's probably fitter than the others, more experienced than the twenty-year-olds."

"Are you being ageist?"

"No, I'm stating a fact."

"Where did you get this fact from?"

"You're in your forties. Are you fit enough to murder two teenage girls, remove their feet and dispose of them without getting caught?"

He shrugged. "Probably not. But there are guys in their eighties who still pump iron, Maria. I think we just need to work our way through the list and tick them off."

"Fine, but we need to do it on the way to speak to Stanley. If he can tell us what happened before, it might help now."

"You think we have a copycat killer?"

"I know we do. It's been bothering me, the foot thing. I remember the case from way back in the day when I was growing up. My mom always used to talk about it; she was a little obsessed with seventies serial killers."

"Well, now's the time to call your sugar daddy and ask him to get someone on the research to save us time."

"He's not my sugar daddy."

Frankie shrugged as he shoved half a bagel into his mouth, leaving him unable to answer her while he chewed. Maria took out her phone and messaged Harrison. Seconds after she pressed send, her phone rang.

"Maria, how are you feeling?"

"Better, thanks. I appreciate the closet full of clothes. Estha has good taste, although some of the items I can't wear for work. They are far too good for that, so I'll get her to take them back."

"Can you wear them out of work?"

Maria thought about the Chanel jackets and pumps, the luxurious feel of the material, and replied. "Yes, but—"

"No buts. If they are to your taste, then I want you to keep them."

"Thank you, I appreciate it. I can't remember the last time I bought new clothes and never that kind of quality."

"Maybe when you're not so busy we could go shopping together. I could get the staff to fawn over you like in *Pretty Woman*."

Laughing, she shook her head. "You watched it then?"

"I read the reviews and asked Estha about it. She told me the entire story while making me supper. I can be your Edward if you'll be my Vivian."

Maria, who had taken a sip of the fresh coffee, spat it all down herself. "I'm not a hooker. I'm a cop."

Harrison laughed. "No, you aren't. You have very high morals, much to my dismay."

She smiled. "These clothes are more than enough—you're very kind. But look, I'm phoning for a favor."

"Anything."

"Do you have somebody who can look into the history of the Parker for me and Frankie? Do a deep dive right back, any murders, deaths, scandals, that kind of thing. Maybe find out what was on that land before they built the hotel, too."

Frankie arched an eyebrow at her at the same time that Harrison let out a sigh. "It's okay if you can't. That's fine, we can do it ourselves."

"That was a sigh of delight. I have an amazing team of researchers who can most definitely do that for you. You finally feel as if you can trust me and that means more to me than anything, Maria. Leave it with me. If you guys need anything, Estha will get it. She's wonderful so please don't give her a hard time."

"I would do no such thing, thank you."

She ended the call, a smile spreading across her lips. "He's on it. Have we got footage of the girls arriving at the bus station?"

"No, I haven't trawled through that yet. Seeing as how they walked into the Parker on their own, I don't think anybody met them at the bus station."

"I agree. I think Dory was in contact with someone from the hotel. We need her cell, laptop, iPad, whatever electronics she had. We need to find who she was talking to and what the plan was for the girls when they arrived. They only had backpacks, no cases, so it was a short visit. Dory had an unhealthy interest in room 1303. Maybe she wanted to look around it, record some stuff, then was going to head home before either girl's parents realized."

Frankie nodded. "Sounds right to me."

Maria stood up. "I think Dory trusted whoever she was in contact with enough to follow their instructions. I don't think this was a disorganized kill. He had everything planned out. He lured them there, knowing all along he was going to kill them. He didn't think that someone would find the room so quickly and put out the fire, which must have thrown him and upset his routine. It makes me so mad that he did this to them. Come on, let's go see Stanley. See what he has to tell us about that place and why it has such a hold over people."

Frankie stuffed the rest of his bagel into his mouth, then downed his coffee and followed her into Harrison's private elevator. Even though this place was upmarket and well-lit, not full of shadows like the Parker, Maria was glad she didn't have to go out into the hallways. The red brick and cast-iron facade of the Parker stirred a deep-seated fear inside her gut—one she didn't think she'd ever be able to push to one side.

NINETEEN

Shore View Tower Apartments lived up to its name. If Maria was going to retire, it would be near a beach but not too far from the city, and this could be the place. Frankie squinted up at the apartments, a hand cupped over his brow to block out the harsh winter sun that blinded the pair of them.

"How much do you reckon these cost? Affordable on our pay scale? Because I'd like to slum it out here. Look, the beach and boardwalk are only across the way. I could eat at Nathan's Hot Dogs every day and talk to the gulls."

Maria stared at him. "Are you going soft, Frankie?" An image of him in board shorts and a loud Hawaiian shirt, wearing a straw trilby, filled her mind, and she liked it. Though she'd miss him, she'd like to see Frankie taking it easy and enjoying life. He'd worked hard, and the city streets were as mean as they come.

"What are you smiling at?"

"You. I was thinking how this lifestyle would suit you just perfect."

He winked. "You could get sugar daddy to buy you one, too."

"Stop calling him that. He is not my sugar daddy."

"No, but he wants to be. Scratch that, I take it back. I think he wants to be a lot more than that. If you want some advice, I'd take anything he offers you seriously. This job is aging you. Do you really want to keep fighting demons and scary stuff? What were we thinking agreeing to this?"

Maria knew Frankie meant well, even if what he said sounded insulting. She didn't want to face the scary stuff she'd dealt with up to now ever again. Yet, she'd signed up to do just that. Now she was being plagued in her nightmares by some evil shadow man who lived in the Parker. He'd almost killed her in a dream by stabbing her. What else could he do when she was at her most vulnerable?

Frankie leaned forward and pressed the intercom for Stanley's apartment. The entrance doors clicked, and he pushed them open. The apartment was light and airy, and Maria thought it seemed a happy place to live. She didn't pick up on any bad vibes, which was nice because lately, almost everywhere she set foot in made her skin prickle.

A short, bald-headed guy waited in a doorway. He wore board shorts and a vivid purple Hawaiian shirt with loud splashes of yellow all over it. It was as if her vision of a retired Frankie had been brought to life.

He grinned at them, and Maria heard herself say, "Stanley?"

"The one and only. Come on in and let me get you both a drink."

Frankie went first and Maria followed, wondering what this conversation was going to bring to their investigation. The thought of what he might be about to disclose to them both perturbed her.

Inside, the apartment was like a discotheque from the seventies. Neon-pink signs hung on the wall. One said *Cocktails*, while another read *Stan's Bar*. The walls were painted white, and black and white prints of a bustling hotel reception hung behind a long gold bar that filled the entire length of one wall. Stanley pointed towards one of six bar stools. "Take a load off. I suppose you're on duty so won't want anything that has alcohol?"

Maria stared up at the huge, gold disco ball above the bar. "No, water is fine. Thank you."

He nodded. "You like this place?"

Despite it not being her taste at all, Maria found that she did. "I love it, Stanley. It's so seventies and kitsch."

A roar of laughter filled the room and Stanley slapped his thigh. "Thank you. It's loud but I'm proud of it. I always loved the old discotheque down in the basement of the Parker and decided long ago that when I had my own place, I would create my own version of it. I rescued a lot of this stuff when the builders came in and tore the old Parker discotheque apart. Kept it stored until the day I got this place. I've had some great parties in here, some real good times." He lovingly ran his hand along the top of the bar. "Some amazing people sat at this bar back in the day. Marilyn Monroe sipped cocktails on one of those stools you're sitting on. You name a celebrity, and I can tell you if they drank at the Parker."

At the mention of Marilyn Monroe, Maria felt a tear pool in the corner of her eye. She'd had the pleasure of meeting her for the briefest of moments when she'd travelled back in time to save Riley Holt, which had left her with such a profound feeling of love for the woman. Frankie's voice brought her back to the present.

"I'm afraid we're here about bad times at the hotel. Have you heard about the double murder of two teen girls?"

Stanley nodded. "I monitor everything that happens at the Parker, and I was so sorry to read about that. It's tragic and a waste of such young lives. Have you caught the perp?"

Maria shook her head. She had so many questions for the

man standing behind the bar, looking like a much older version of Tom Cruise in *Cocktail*. "I wish we had, but not yet."

Frankie interjected, "We have some interesting leads, though. If we show you a list of names, would you remember if any of them worked at the hotel when you were still there?"

"Sure, sure. I never forget a name."

Frankie collected the print-out of seven names from his bag and passed it to Stanley, who took a pair of reading glasses out of his pocket. He peered at the list.

"Manuel has been there almost as long as I was. Good guy, he's not who you would be looking for. Neither are Darius, John, Alexander, or Lucas. They're good workers, too. Never caused any problems for me, or any reason to be concerned about their behavior. I can't vouch for the other two. They must have started after I retired. Henry and Elijah, I've never heard of." He passed the sheet back and Maria took it from him, putting an asterisk next to Harry and Elijah's names. They were aged twenty-nine and thirty-eight.

"They were found on the thirteenth floor," Frankie told him, and Stanley shook his head.

"Let me guess, you found them in room 1303? Am I right?"

Maria glanced at Frankie and nodded. "What makes you think of that room first?"

He passed them both bottles of Evian from the cooler behind the bar and poured himself a large glass of bourbon, adding lots of ice. "Are you sure you wouldn't like something a bit stronger?"

She noticed Frankie lick his lips at the sight of the amber liquid sloshing against the cut-glass tumbler Stanley placed on the bar, but he shook his head. "No, we're good for now. Thanks."

Stanley pulled out one of the stools from behind the bar and sat opposite them. "That goddamn room needs locking up and the key throwing away. It's a bad, bad room. Every hotel has a room that is supposed to be haunted but that one... it's more than that. It's always had this vibe, this sense of something not being right inside it. Worse than some ordinary ghost, if you get what I mean. I guess it started way back in the day when the hotel first opened. A businessman from out of town was murdered in that room. His money was stolen. It was brutal by what I was told. The killer beat him so bad about the head he couldn't be identified by his next of kin."

"When was this?"

"1884."

"Oh, I had no idea the hotel was so old."

He nodded at Maria. "During my time at the hotel, every few years someone died in that room. At one point I locked it up and stopped renting it out to guests. I couldn't take the guilt or the worrying about when it would happen again. Especially after what happened with Gabriella. It was safer for everyone that way. But new management came in, updated it and I had to open it up again."

"When was this?"

"1979. It was only in use for a couple of months when that monster killed those two women and cut off their feet. He set fire to it, but it didn't burn. I'm telling you I had nightmares for months about those poor women. The cops had no idea who'd done it. We didn't have cameras back then; guests could give false names, and nobody knew any different. A month later, there was another attempted murder. Room 1303 had only been in use a couple of days when it happened again. This woman was lucky—she survived and only lost a foot."

Frankie spat out the mouthful of water down the front of his shirt. Maria felt cold, creeping fingers of fear trailing up her spine.

"Same guy?"

Stanley shrugged. "No idea. Different name but same... what do you call it? The same M.O. We didn't get too many guests cutting off women's feet for fun. The victim was in a bad way. Stayed in hospital for some time, and she didn't have health insurance. She was a regular in the bar downstairs. Cherry, her name was. She was a hooker. Most of the girls who hung around the hotel were, and I didn't give a damn. As long as they didn't rip the guests off and were fair, I let them use the bar. It was safer for them there than out on the streets. Wasn't too safe for poor Cherry, though. I felt bad about that. I told the hospital she was staff and added her onto our paperwork, so the hotel paid her medical bills. Thought I'd lose my job over that one, but nobody ever found out."

Maria was scribbling all of this down. "Is Cherry still around? Would you know how to get hold of her?"

"I couldn't say. I have her real name in my book. I'll get it for you before you leave."

Frankie said, "I vaguely remember hearing about this case."

"Management paid the press to keep it low key, said they didn't need the bad publicity."

Maria looked up. "Did they catch the killer?"

Stanley shook his head. "No, he disappeared without a trace. There was speculation that he was one of my employees. I'm telling you now, he wasn't. I would have known. Besides, if he'd worked at the Parker, it would have happened again. After the failed murder of Cherry, there were no more killings. I kept an eye on the press to see if maybe he moved on to a different part of town, even the country. Nothing like that ever happened again. He either got caught for another crime and put in prison, or he died. Somebody capable of that was never going to stop and go back to their normal lives. They never found the women's feet either."

Maria thought about the creepy, shadow guy who had chased her through her dream. "Do you think he could have hidden the feet in the hotel? Or could he have died in the hotel?" Maybe he'd killed himself in a place where nobody could find him.

"I don't think so. We'd have smelled his body, or the staff would have. Where would he hide two pairs of feet without one of the maids coming across them? Not to be disrespectful but they would have smelled bad. It's the kind of smell that seeps into everything, as I'm sure you guys know."

Maria did—they both did. It was hard to get rid of the smell of decomposition once you came into contact with it.

"Did anyone give you a name?"

"Cherry said the guy was called Arnie. He was on a business trip and that's about all she could remember. Before you ask, I checked the guest register. We had a guy in room 1303 but he wasn't called Arnie. He was called David Jones. He never checked out. I gave the police his details and they visited his wife who told them he was a traveling salesman. They kept waiting for him to turn up, but he didn't, as far as I know. I'm certain he was the guy, but I have no idea what happened to him or where he went after that."

Maria underlined the name David Jones a couple of times. "Rick told us you kept a blue book to record strange incidents in the hotel. Do you still have it?"

Stanley crossed his arms, uncrossed them, and picked up his glass, draining the bourbon before answering them. "Yeah, I do, but why are you asking about that?"

Maria decided to be truthful. He had been open and honest with them up to now.

"When we first got called to the crime scene, I saw somebody up on the tenth floor. They were looking down at the street and were dressed in blue."

He looked at her. Maria could feel tiny beads of perspiration on her brow. She knew she wasn't looking her best. She'd put her coldness down to fear, but it could also have been the infection in her wound making her ill again.

"What happened to you? Are you sick? Because you look kind of sick."

"I got stabbed in my back and it's infected. I'm better than I was but if I'm being honest with you, I don't feel too good. But please carry on... the woman in blue..."

Stanley had a look of sadness in his eyes. "I never saw her; plenty of people did. Staff, guests... but it was never a good thing for anyone to see her. I'm sorry that you are sick, that you got hurt. Who stabbed you?"

Frankie watched her, his lips parted as if he was going to say something to stop her from talking, but she placed her hand gently on his arm.

"This is going to sound insane, but it's what happened. After we left the hotel for the first time, I went out for a couple of drinks with my friend. I fell asleep and had the worst, most terrifying nightmare I've ever had. I was back in the hotel on the thirteenth floor. The door to room 1303 was open when it shouldn't have been. As I went to enter, a shadow appeared on the wall. It was evil, I know that it was. And it chased me. I ran for the elevator, and as I got inside, I felt a sharp pain in my shoulder blade. That's when I woke up, thrashing around in a bed in the Plaza, with a deep wound on my shoulder. My friend said it was probably the bed spring. The manager replaced the mattress, and then I got sick."

"Do you think it was the bed spring? I've run a hotel for many years and never had that happen to a guest. I can't imagine the Plaza has either. I mean, it's the freakin' Plaza, you know?"

Stanley stood up. He left the room, and they heard him moving stuff around. Frankie stared at Maria. She let him. What could she say? She'd spoken the truth. No, she didn't think her injury was caused by the bed spring. Whoever chased her in the dream managed to stab her. Stanley came back with a blue leather book clutched to his chest. He let it drop onto the bar in front of Maria with a loud thud.

"I never heard that one before—a shadow guy chasing folk down and hurting them. You can take the book. Add your story to it and when you're done with it bring it back. There's a lot in there, too much for me to talk about. But it contains every incident that guests or staff ever reported to me of a supernatural nature."

Maria stared at the book. She'd expected a small journal, not a huge book the size of an old-fashioned family bible.

"They say that anyone who sees the woman in blue is in trouble. They'll die or someone close to them will. But if you got stabbed, then got sick, but survived, you should be okay. That was your brush with death, and you fought it. Now, I don't know how or why, because it doesn't usually happen that way, but maybe God has a plan for you, detective. Maybe he needs you here to fight his good fight against all things bad in this world. If he didn't, then you wouldn't be here talking to me about stuff that we both know has no business existing. But we are here."

He smiled. "The Parker was my life for so long and I love that place, but it had a hold over me that made it almost impossible to leave. I was glad when Covid came along and forced it to close. It gave me the chance to get out while I could. Read the book, take from it what you can. Some of the stories are probably rubbish and not worth the effort, but some are worth looking into. A lot of guests reported nightmares and bad dreams, especially up on the thirteenth. They might help you figure out what the hell is happening to you—and in the hotel."

Maria nodded. "Thank you. I, we, appreciate your help, Stanley." Her mouth was dry as she uncapped the bottle of water and glugged down half in one mouthful. "Would you have any Tylenol?"

He bent under the bar and passed her a huge white bottle

with a red lid. "Help yourself." Then he turned to Frankie. "I think your colleague should go home and rest. Maybe take it easy for a couple of days. I'm no doctor, but she shouldn't be out chasing killers and whatever else while she's running a fever."

Maria shook her head. "I'm good, or I will be when these kick in." She popped three into her mouth and washed them down with the rest of the water. She was not going to collapse in Stanley's apartment, that was for sure. Even though her legs felt wobbly, she could make it out to the car. She needed to talk to Missy and Emilia about what had happened to her. They could help—she was sure of that.

TWENTY

"Can you take me to the Plaza?" Maria was huddled in the front of the car. The heating blasted out, warming her bones that were both frozen and on fire at the same time.

"I thought you were stopping at the towers?"

"I don't know where I'm stopping, but I have to speak to Henry the manager—like now." She felt bad for snapping at Frankie but was too tired to argue with him. He must have realized, because he nodded and didn't answer back.

Traffic was bad all the way there. She wanted to get this over with then go home to sleep for a while. Frankie pulled up to the curb, and she jumped out. "Wait here."

He didn't argue with her, and she knew he was a little put out at the way she'd talked to him. She'd make it up to him when she felt better.

The entrance was busy, there were tourists everywhere. She had to cut through them to get to the desk. She'd no idea if Henry would even be on duty. To her relief, she saw him talking to a guest. He spotted her, excused himself and rushed over to her.

"Ms. Miller, is everything okay? You don't look so good?"

She shook her head. "My shoulder, it's infected."

The look of horror that crossed his face told her he was thinking about lawsuits and whatever else could be thrown the Plaza's way. He took hold of her elbow and gently guided her to the manager's office. "I'm so sorry, let me get you a medic."

She held up her hand. "Henry, none of this is your fault and I'm not blaming the hotel. That's not why I'm here."

His shoulders dropped and he let out a sigh of relief.

"I need you to be honest with me. Did you check... was there a loose spring in that mattress?"

"I don't know, Ms. Miller. I had it taken away and replaced immediately."

"Not Ms. Miller. Maria, please. Can you show it to me? I need to see it."

He nodded. "Yes, we can do that, of course. Come with me."

He offered her his arm. Normally she wouldn't have accepted, but she liked Henry, so she linked hers through his. "You have a fever, Maria, you're burning up."

"I know. I've had some Tylenol. It will be fine as soon as they kick in."

He took her to the staff elevator and pressed the lower basement button. When the doors opened, the blast of cool air was a welcome relief. He led her along a corridor until he reached a door and swiped his card to get inside. The lights came on and she saw pallets of new mattresses stacked up. There was one mattress to the side without plastic sheeting around it and a note that read *Penthouse* taped to it.

"Maintenance left it here in case there were any repercussions."

Maria walked across to look at it. The side facing her was perfect. Running her hand along the soft material, she could feel nothing sharp. There was clearly nothing sticking out of it. "Can we flip it?"

Henry rushed over and took hold of it, pulling it away from the wall so Maria could see the other side. It was perfect: there wasn't anything sticking through the material, no springs, nothing that could have caused her injury. A wave of nausea rose up from her stomach and she had to cup a hand across her mouth. She told herself she was good, she wasn't going to puke, not here in front of Henry, who'd done everything to help her that he could.

She swallowed the bile back down and smiled at him. "Thank you. I'm sorry for being an asshole."

"Maria, you are not an asshole. I don't know what happened with your shoulder but I'm sorry you got hurt. Is there anything I can do to help? There must be something."

She shook her head. "No, thanks. This is my mess and I'll clear it up one way or another. Thanks for the offer, though. You're the best. Oh, there is one thing."

"Anything."

"Don't tell Mr. Williams I was here asking about the bed; I don't want to upset him."

"Of course not, Maria. Discretion is my specialty. It has to be in this business. If I see a guest bring back a friend for an evening, then his wife turns up the next day, you better believe I'll have someone up to that room to help them clear up the problem. It's shady, but it's part of the job. Same with some of the ladies who frequent here. They like a little fun while their husbands are out of town, and we don't want to cause trouble for anyone."

Maria couldn't help what was about to come out of her mouth, even though she knew it was none of her business. "Do you have to clean up Mr. Harrison's messes often?"

"Never. He's a true gentleman and I can honestly say one of the nicest guys I've had the pleasure of taking care of."

"He is, huh? I kinda get that. I don't see what he finds so

great about me when he could have anybody he wants—well, practically."

"Ah, may I be so bold as to explain this situation?"

"Yes."

"He sees a strong, independent woman who can take care of herself and others without expecting anything in return. He knows you're not shallow, that you don't care whether he has money or not, and he, I suspect, loves you for all those reasons. Some of his other partners have been... how do I put this without sounding harsh? Not like you, they *did* care about the money. They were shallow, and can I say that they were as entitled as you would expect a member of the British monarchy to be? They may have looked like trophies on the outside, but on the inside, they were quite awful.

"It's not for me to give advice to anyone, but you are as much of an equal to Mr. Harrison as anyone, and he respects you for that. What you need to remember is, we are all equals regardless of our station in life. Some people have money, others have none. What matters, at the end of the day, is how you treat people. You could be the poorest person in the country, but if you are kind and respectful to others, it makes you an awful lot richer than most."

Tears pricked at the corner of her eyes. "Thank you, Henry."

"My pleasure. I would ask yourself if there was no money involved, would you find him a fun guy to date?"

She nodded.

"Then there's your answer."

The bright lights of the foyer hurt Maria's eyes as the elevator doors slid open.

"Thank you."

"You are most welcome. Maria, please take care of yourself. If you need to rest, I can get you a key for the suite and you can take it easy, order some room service, and let yourself feel better."

"I would love that. It would make me feel like Kevin in *Home Alone*, but I have a bad guy to catch, and I can't do that eating ice cream, feeling sorry for myself."

Henry laughed. "True. Have a wonderful day, Ms. Miller, and do wrap up warm. It's awfully cold outside." He spoke in his best Tim Curry voice and gave her a little bow.

She grinned, appreciating the impression—*Home Alone* was one of her favorite Christmas movies. She winked at him, hurrying back out to find Frankie who would no doubt be raging at how long she'd been. At least she knew the truth. The bed hadn't hurt her. It had been that creepy, shadow guy. If he was hanging around in the Parker, haunting people's dreams, he was powerful. She needed to find a way to stop him while finding the killer at the same time. And to do that, she needed to feel a lot better than she did right now.

TWENTY-ONE

They talked until Cherry could no longer keep her eyes open. The warmth in the room combined with the alcohol they'd consumed made her sleepy. She lay slumped on the bed and began to snore ever so gently. He stared at her, wishing that he didn't have to do what he was planning. But he had no choice. A fire burning inside him compelled him to do it. Besides, another opportunity might not present itself so willingly. He would be foolish to let it slide.

She really was a good-looking woman, underneath that baby blue eyeshadow and red lips. She was fun to talk to, too, not like his wife, who was so straight-up boring she could kill someone by droning on about the most uninteresting subjects you could imagine. He gently slid off her shoes and held the shiny, cheap, red patent leather to his nose, inhaling deeply. The smell of her feet wasn't unpleasant, mingled with the smell from the shoe. He felt his mind go blank as he let out a groan.

He could take her shoes, leave her sleeping, and go find another woman. He was tempted to do just that, but she already knew who he was. She'd be able to give a good description to the cops and before he knew it, his face would be all over the news channels. His wife, who watched the news religiously, would recognize him and phone the cops. It would be game over. A tiny part of him thought that maybe that would be a good thing. He was sick in the head; he knew that, but couldn't do anything about it.

He opened his case and took out the rope and the bone saw. He'd picked it up at the butcher's one day when the guy working there was out the back. He'd popped it into his grocery sack without a second thought. It was perfect; it did the job quickly and efficiently, saving him hacking through with an axe.

He felt as if he was in a dream. A miniature version of himself sat on one shoulder, pitchfork and horns on his head, telling him to stop being a baby and get it over with. On the other was his goddamn wife wearing wings with a shiny halo, telling him to be a good man. But he could feel darkness take over him. The devil was winning this battle.

Movement in the corner of the room caught his eye. He whipped around to see a black shadow on the opposite wall. Or at least it looked like a shadow—but that was impossible, because it had moved when he was standing completely still. He shook his head and instantly regretted it; the bourbon had given him nothing but a headache. As he moved the bone saw slowly, the shadow in the corner remained still. Puzzled, he attributed what he was seeing to the alcohol he'd drunk and his active imagination. Then the shadow moved again. This time, he knew he'd kept completely still.

Confused and more than a little bit scared, he wondered if Cherry had slipped a little acid in his bourbon. Wouldn't that be a plot twist? He'd wanted to get her drunk to kill her and she'd sent him tripping, making him literally scared of his own shadow. Unsure what was happening, he sighed. His breath fogged up the air in front of him. He hadn't realized just how cold it was in this room.

He turned in slow motion, checking each wall to see where

his shadow had gone. What happened when your shadow escaped? Could you live without it? Did it take on a life of its own and become its own entity? He'd never really thought about it. Then again, he didn't know if he was tripping because he'd never done drugs. They didn't appeal to him, unlike losing himself in a bottle of Jack Daniels.

Cherry let out a snort on the bed, bringing his attention back to her and the whole reason he was here. He still had one of her shoes clutched in his hand. He took out a quarter and flipped it in the air. It landed with a tiny thwack on the back of his hand. *Heads you live, tails you die*, he whispered. Uncovering the coin, he looked down at George Washington. *You live.*

He felt relieved she was going to make it to see another day. But the black shadow had other ideas. It lunged off the wall, making him scream out in fear. He was aware of the feeling of being crushed, as if the thing was trying to mold itself into him, and he wrestled with it, to no avail. It began to dissolve into him, as if his body was absorbing it. His mouth was full of darkness that tasted like hell. Looking into the mirror, he saw the shadow melt into him, becoming one with him. He opened his mouth to scream but nothing came out, except for thick, black smoke that choked his voice completely.

Cherry stirred on the bed. He wanted to call out to her to help him, but he couldn't. He watched on as his own hand lifted the bone saw. His feet moved in a jerky, uncontrolled way towards her body. Her pantyhose was on the floor, and he stooped, picking them up, and wrapped them around her neck. Her eyes flew open. She stared blankly at him, until the pressure got too much, and she lost consciousness. He didn't know if she was dead or only out cold, but it didn't matter. He couldn't stop himself, no matter how hard he tried.

Next thing he knew, the saw was cutting through the soft flesh of her ankle. He could hear scraping as the saw connected with bone. He realized with a sense of sadness that Cherry must be dead because there was no way she could be alive and not screaming the place down. It was over in a couple of minutes; he held up her foot in one hand. He dropped the bloodied saw onto the bed next to her.

Seconds later, he found himself standing, in some kind of daze, in front of the wall where the shadow had leapt from. He reached out to touch the wall, placing a heavily bloodstained hand onto it as he sucked in the coppery-tinged air, trying to snap himself out of whatever dream-like state he was in. That was the only way he could describe it. He felt as if he'd woken in the middle of the worst nightmare of his life. Then he felt a tremendous pressure as his hand was pulled and tugged into the drywall.

Pain hit him—burning, white-hot pain, as his arm disappeared. He opened his mouth to scream, but the next moment his entire body was being dragged into the wall by a great invisible force. He could taste the plaster, the dust. It felt as if he was being slowly crushed to death and there was nothing he could do about it. His body merged completely into the wall, leaving nothing behind but the bloodied handprint.

On the bed, Cherry woke. She screamed over and over, wondering what the hell had just happened. The blinding pain from where her foot had been hacked off took over, sending her body into shock. She heard hammering on the door, but there was nothing she could do about it. She felt as if she was dying and realized that death would be a welcome relief from this raw, nightmarish pain. The door was kicked through from the outside, and then she passed out.

TWENTY-TWO

"What's the deal? What took you so long?"

Frankie looked pissed as she got into the car. "Sorry, I had to speak to the manager. Can you take me home? I need to speak to Missy."

"What is this? Maria's limousine?"

She didn't answer.

Frankie swung the car around to a cacophony of blaring horns. He gave the drivers the finger as he sped down 5th Avenue. The shops went past in a blur. When he reached Saint Patrick's, Maria had an urge to go inside the beautiful cathedral and wondered why. She wasn't a particularly religious person—although she was beginning to realize that God, whether she wanted to believe or not, did have a part to play in some of what they had dealt with previously.

She wondered how Mikey was. He'd helped them to fight the demon in the house on West 10th Street and hoped he was doing good. He worked as a security guard in the cathedral. Then there was Father Tony. Maybe she should tell him about her bad dreams and ask him to bless her. It couldn't hurt. But before she could ask Frankie to stop, they'd already passed, and were somehow managing to beat the red lights to get her home. He pulled up by the curb outside her apartment and turned to her. "Now what?"

"I'm going to speak to Missy and then have a cold shower. I'm too hot. Grab an hour's rest, then we'll meet in a couple of hours. Is that fine with you?"

He nodded. "Yeah, I'm good with that. Should I come in with you? I'm worried about you."

He didn't add that she looked like crap, and she smiled at him. "I'm good, just need to cool down and put some fresh clothes on, but thanks, Frankie."

He didn't look convinced. "Call me when you're ready to be picked up."

She got out of the car, with Stanley's blue book tucked under her good arm. Her body felt sluggish. She forced herself to smile at Frankie, and he lifted a hand, then pulled out while there was a gap in the traffic.

Missy opened the door, took one look at Maria and yelled, "Emilia."

"I'm not contagious, just sick."

Missy hooked an arm around Maria's. "Yes, you are sick. Why are you here and not at the ER?"

"Been there, got the meds and a tetanus shot. I need your advice."

When Emilia saw Maria's pale, clammy complexion, her eyes opened wide. She stepped to one side to let the women into the lounge. "What happened, dear?" Emilia took hold of her arm and helped Maria onto the couch then lifted the back of her hand to feel her forehead. "You have a fever."

Emilia went to the bathroom and came back with a bottle of Advil. She passed her two and Missy brought her a glass of iced lemonade. Maria took the tablets and downed the drink, which tasted like liquid heaven. She smiled at her two elderly neighbors and wondered why she kept coming to them for help, knowing full well that each time she was involving them in something dark and unnatural. She opened her mouth to tell them she was okay and felt hot tears trickle down her cheeks. Both women gasped and rushed to her, sitting either side, taking hold of a hand each.

"Is it Frankie?" asked Missy.

"Did Harrison break up with you, honey?" asked Emilia.

Maria shook her head. Emilia passed her a Kleenex and she wiped her tears then blew her nose.

"They're both okay, and no, he hasn't broken up with me yet."

"Then what is it? You can tell us anything, you know that."

Maria clasped their hands tight, squeezing a little. "I know. I'm sorry I bothered you both, I just feel really sick and it's making me act all weird."

"How did you get sick?" Missy watched her face carefully.

"I got an injury on my shoulder in a dream and it's infected."

"Can I see it?"

Maria shrugged off her jacket and unbuttoned her shirt enough so she could slip an arm out of one sleeve. "You might want to wear gloves. I don't want you catching anything." Maria knew, though, that what she had wasn't catching; it was some kind of evil that had been put into her body like a poison. Missy fetched a pair of plastic gloves from the kitchen and tugged them on, then gently peeled back the dressing. She didn't say a word, but Emilia gasped in horror. "Oh dear, we need to get you to the ER."

"I've been, they cleaned it."

Missy went to the sink. They had a boiling water faucet and she filled a bowl up with it, placing it on the side to cool a little.

"What kind of dream did you get hurt in? Was it a bad one?"

"Yes."

"I need you to tell me about it, but first I need to call a friend while this water cools. Excuse me." Missy disappeared into the bedroom.

"Who is she calling?" asked Maria.

"I have no idea," Emilia replied. "I didn't think she had any friends except for the two of us."

Maria smiled then whispered, "I'm scared to sleep in case it happens again, but I'm so tired."

"Then we'll get you cleaned up and you can sleep here. We will watch you to make sure you're not having a nightmare and if you are we can wake you up before anything happens."

Emilia hugged her as tenderly as she could, and Maria thanked God that she was lucky enough to have these two beautiful souls in her life. She didn't know how she would survive without them.

"Thank you."

Missy came back in. "He's on his way, but for now let me try to clean it as best as I can. While I'm doing that, you can explain to me what sort of dream you had. Actually, let's hang on so you don't have to do it twice."

Maria nodded. She could feel her eyelids beginning to droop. The warmth of the room, the comfort of her two friends being close by, and knowing they would wake her if anything bad happened, lulled her into a sense of security, and she lay down on her side. She slipped into a slumber that took her away from this world and into another.

But she didn't go back to the Parker. This time as she slept, Maria saw a darkness so consuming she couldn't see or hear anything except the whisper of voices in the distance. Her eyelids fluttered open and for a moment she had no idea where she was, until she saw Emilia's concerned face watching her from the chair opposite. The whispers stopped and she realized the voices were Missy and a man, judging by the deep tone of his voice. Maria sat up, mortified that she had passed out like that.

"I'm sorry."

Emilia shook her head. "Don't you dare be sorry. I watched you to make sure you were okay. You didn't look as if you were having a nightmare."

"No, you looked as if you were dead," said Missy.

Maria turned and saw Missy drinking a glass of lemonade. Beside her, dressed in a pair of faded jeans and a black shirt with a starched white clerical collar, was Father Anthony. He smiled at Maria.

"It's good to see you, Detective Miller. It's been too long."

Confusion took over, and Missy stepped in. "I think what you need is cleansing, and Father Anthony happened to be in the neighborhood. Now, do you feel up to telling us about your nightmare that caused all of this?"

Maria didn't have the energy to argue. She simply stated the facts as the three of them listened, wide-eyed and open-mouthed. It was Father Anthony who talked first.

"You were attacked, during a nightmare, in the Parker Hotel? A shadow figure chased you to the lift and that shadow figure somehow managed to stab you with a knife?"

If Maria was listening to a victim tell her this, she'd be struggling to contain an eye roll. "Yes."

He nodded. "There wasn't anything that you could have injured yourself with in the bed? Or in the room? The corner of a table? A shard of broken glass?"

"Nothing. I've been back to the Plaza to look at the mattress. We thought maybe a spring had come through, but it was perfect."

Missy pointed to her shoulder. "I think you should take a

look at it. I'm not sure what happened but something did, and it's infected her."

He stood up. "Yes, absolutely."

Maria let the soft blanket that either Missy or Emilia had covered her with drop so he could see the wound. As he walked around, he let out a small gasp. "Oh, my. That looks painful. Did the ER not give you a shot and some antibiotics?"

"I've had everything including Tylenol, Advil, antibiotics and a tetanus shot."

Father Anthony smiled at her. "Well, you haven't had this. Are you okay for me to bathe it with some fresh holy water straight out of the font at St Patrick's?"

"At this point, you could bathe it in acid if it makes it clean and gets rid of this sickness." Maria laughed, but she was being serious.

Father Anthony pulled a bottle of Evian out of his bag, and Maria arched an eyebrow. "I didn't have a container big enough. It's clean. Maria, how is your faith? I know that you struggle with the whole God and Jesus thing, but after the epic battle in the house on West 10th Street, do you feel a little different? I really need you to give into it as much as you can."

He stared deep into her eyes, and Maria felt heat spread across her cheeks. He was so young, so handsome. He'd sacrificed so much to serve God, when there were so many things he could do with his life. But he was the perfect man for the job.

"It's much stronger than it's ever been, thanks to you. I'm not sure it's at the stage where I'm a devoted follower, though, and want to go to church regularly, but I do believe in the goodness and light God and Jesus bring into the darkest days of our lives. I know they are all around us if we let them in. I just don't always let them hang around if you get what I mean."

He bent over double as deep laughter filled the room. It took him a minute to compose himself. "You should have been a comedian, Maria. You missed your way. I don't need you to be at my level of belief but need you to have some comprehension of what it means to believe in the good man, and that's a pretty decent way to look at it. I think you'll be okay, if you keep seeing things like that."

He took out a large crucifix, which he hung around his neck, then his silk stole and a solid silver cross. Placing them on the coffee table, he smiled at them all.

"Shall we pray?"

Father Andrew held out his hand to Maria and she took it, feeling instantly calmer. Missy took his other hand and Emilia sealed the circle. They looked a strange sight, the two senior women, a priest and the sick detective all holding hands in a circle. He began to pray to Saint Michael the archangel, asking him for protection. Maria closed her eyes and let his warm words wash over her. He murmured *amen* and broke the circle, clapping his hands. "Right, are you ready, Maria? I'm afraid that this may hurt, or it might not. This isn't something I've come across before. It's a learning curve for us all. Father Morgan suggested it."

Missy rolled her eyes. "That old goat is full of surprises."

Father Anthony nodded.

"I don't care if it hurts. I just want this sickness to go. I have a killer to catch, and I can't focus feeling like this. I'm ready, please do it."

He picked up the silver crucifix and the water. Maria turned so he could get to her shoulder. Uncapping the bottle of water, Missy held a hand towel below the wound to catch the excess. Father Anthony began to pray again as he poured the cool liquid on the wound. Maria had to stifle a cry of pain that racked her entire shoulder. It felt as if it was on fire, the pain was so blinding and intense. She could smell the stench of burning flesh and realized—with horror—it was her own. Her teeth gritted as she felt the cool steel of the silver crucifix being pressed across the wound and gradually the heat began to subside. The wound was still throbbing, but it was more bearable now, and the water started to cool the flesh around it. Emilia had a tight hold of her hand.

Maria squeezed back and, through gritted teeth, she whispered, "It's okay, I'm good."

Even though her skin was tingling, her shoulder felt better than it had in days. Maria didn't feel as sick. The last of the water trickled down her back and Maria let out the breath she'd been holding in. Missy clapped her hands. "Well, I'll be damned, that looks better already. The redness has gone. Go take a look, Maria, in the bathroom mirror."

Maria did just that, and as she peered over her shoulder at what had been a burning mess of infection, she saw only a scratch. She whispered, *Thank you, God, I owe you one.* Father Anthony smiled at her as she walked back into the living room. "Thank you."

He nodded. "My pleasure. Now, what are we going to do about the problem at the Parker? I don't want anyone else getting sick like you were."

And Maria felt the heaviness she had been carrying lift from her shoulders. He was going to help her, help them. She thanked God again, this time for sending Anthony to her. He was like her very own guardian angel, and once again she was grateful their paths had crossed.

TWENTY-THREE

After eating a homemade meatball sub smothered in cheese, at Emilia's insistence, Maria took the book Stanley had given her and went to her own apartment next door. It felt as if she'd not been there for days—which, technically, she hadn't—and it felt strange. This jet-setting lifestyle of never sleeping in the same bed was not really her thing. First the Plaza, then the Towers and now home.

She reached out her fingers and let them trail along the hallway. It wasn't much, but it was hers, and someday she'd have enough in her savings account to move to something better. For now, this place served her well enough. Despite what had happened in the apartment, she felt safe there. A blinking blue light on the camera above the door told her she was being monitored. As much as she hated the cameras, she wouldn't risk having them removed. She was the only one with access to the footage, according to Harrison, who'd had them installed. But she didn't believe he couldn't access them if he wanted to. Maria didn't even mind if he did access them; it was nice to know that if she needed help, it could be found.

A cold shiver ran down the length of her spine. She

wasn't going to dwell on what the hell had just happened next door. Doing so would likely send her spiraling into madness. Instead, she went to the bathroom and stripped off her damp shirt and sports bra, tossing them into the laundry hamper. In the mirror, she examined the wound on her shoulder. It was nothing more than a scratch now, yet not an hour ago it had been an angry, red, festering wound making her sicker than she'd ever been. The power of holy water was quite mind blowing. Father Anthony should sell it by the bottle—the water to cure all the bad stuff in your life. Maria smiled at her reflection, and then she felt sad. She looked terrible. The dark circles under her eyes and the pasty complexion didn't suit her. She filled the tub; it seemed that water was good for her soul and a long soak might help her relax.

After her bath, dressed in a pair of leggings and an oversized sweatshirt, her long, dark curls tamed in a messy bun, she made herself a coffee and sat on the couch. Beside her, she'd placed Stanley's blue book. A part of her didn't want to read it; another part was thirsty to know what had happened at the Parker over so many years. Taking a sip of the hot liquid, she closed her eyes and found herself talking out loud.

Hey, I know you're busy and you've already helped me today, for which I am really grateful. Do you think you could spare me a bit more attention, though, and not let anything I read in this book seep under my skin and take a hold of me? I like being me and I like being a cop. I suppose, in a way, I'm helping you out, too, so yeah, a bit of divine protection would be greatly appreciated. Thanks.

She paused as if waiting to hear some kind of angelic choir or something. The only noise was the sound of the cooler kicking in, making her jump, and she laughed. She was losing it.

The sooner she told Addison this department was no longer working for her, the better.

Maria opened the book to the first page. The writing was a messy scrawl and hard to read but she got the gist of it. A guest had seen a shadow moving across the wall when they were in bed reading and demanded another bedroom. She didn't have to be told their room number: it was 1303. That was in 1982, three years after the first double murders, and Maria wondered if this person was the first guest to stay in that room. Scanning the next pages, she read more of the same. A black shadow moved through the walls... cold air... a feeling of something evil... bad dreams... being chased... noises coming from the walls. The entries were short, but they went on and on. Maria stopped reading at the first mention of a woman in a blue dress, staring out of the tenth-floor window. Her cell began to vibrate, making her jump.

"Hey."

"Hey, you, how are you feeling?"

Harrison sounded genuinely concerned. As much as she wanted to tell him everything that had happened, she held back. "I feel much better—the meds must be kicking in."

"Phew. I've been in meetings all afternoon and couldn't call. I'm glad you're feeling better, Maria."

She felt bad lying to him, but it was for his benefit. What was the point in upsetting him about something he had no control over? Despite him being a lovely guy, he liked having control over things.

"Oh, I have some news for you about the Parker. Do you want me to come and see you later when I come out of this next meeting? Or should I mail it over to you?"

"I would love for you to come and see me later, but I need to know what you have as soon as possible. So can you mail it and then we can maybe go for supper or something when you're free."

"Perfect." He paused then lowered his voice. "I have to go, but I love you, Maria."

Maria laughed. "Thanks." Then she hung up the phone.

Saying I love you was probably the hardest sentence she could ever say, and she wasn't ready for that yet. But it warmed Maria's heart to know that he felt that way about her. Maybe she could have a happily ever after. It would be great to see Frankie get his, too. The more she thought about it, the more she realized that his retirement would be good for them both. Instead of them living and breathing down each other's necks, they'd have a little space from each other. If he was dating the doc, he wasn't moping around after her anymore, and despite her initial jealousy, that made her happy.

Maria opened the mail account on her phone and waited for Harrison's email to arrive. When it did, she clicked on the attachment and read the newspaper articles scanned into the document.

The tragic story of the woman in the blue dress who fell from the 10th floor of the Parker in 1945.

Isabelle Winter of Long Island took ill while visiting the ill-fated Parker, a downtown New York hotel which has a long history of strange and unusual deaths. The forty-eight-year-old woman, who was mourning the death of her parents in an automobile accident, had come to the city with her daughter in an effort to cheer themselves up. Mother and daughter checked into the Parker for a four-night stay and, unfortunately, Isabelle never checked out. After an argument about a boy, who Isabelle disliked and who had asked for Faith's hand in marriage, Faith departed to meet a friend, leaving Isabelle alone in their hotel room. Isabelle, a dressmaker by trade, had brought some sewing with her on the trip, along with a pair of sharp fabric shears. In what one can only describe as a fit of madness, she took the shears

and cut off her own hand, and then threw herself out of the
window from the tenth floor. She was wearing a beautiful silk
and taffeta pale blue gown that she had been making for a
customer. Years later, there are sporadic sightings of a woman in
blue on the tenth floor of the Parker Hotel. Rumor has it that if
you catch a glimpse of this ghostly figure, a terrible fate will
befall you. Several people have reported seeing Isabelle's ghost on
the tenth floor, and of those people, many have met tragic deaths.
The manager of the hotel, Stanley Hill, declined to comment.
Have you stayed at the Parker, glimpsed Isabelle's ghost and
lived to tell the tale? If so, kindly inform us of your story by letter.

Maria's heart ached for Isabelle Winter's tragic tale, of a life
that ended with so much loss. She wondered about the reporter
who had written the article and whether anyone had ever been
in touch with stories of their own.

The next attachment was a grainy, colored photo of the
hotel foyer with a tagline that read, ***Double Murder at the
Parker.***

Yesterday, a member of the housekeeping staff made a terrible
discovery as smoke poured underneath the door of room 1303. A
brave resident, who raised the alarm before the housekeeper used
her key to get in, found not one but two dead women sprawled on
the twin beds. Rumor has it they were both missing a foot, but the
NYPD refuse to confirm. Nobody from the hotel was available to
comment at the time of going to print.

Maria was shocked. The article was a tiny sidebar on the
newspaper page. Stanley was right; the hotel management must
have paid the press to keep it quiet. This report must have
slipped through the net. Maria checked the name of the
reporter, Harry Jenks, and wrote it down on a notepad. She
didn't think Harry had anything to tell them, if that was all he

knew, but it was worth speaking to him. After all, they were getting nowhere fast.

The rest of the articles covered suicides. So many guests had gone to the hotel to end their lives, by the time Maria finished reading, she felt drained—not just her energy, but her soul. What lay in the ground under the hotel? What had it been built on to have such an unusually high number of deaths? Maria thanked Harrison over email and asked for his researcher to check if the '79 victim was still alive, and if they could find her address. Harrison messaged back instantly, with one word: *Yes*. While she waited for the address, Maria continued reading the research.

Before the hotel was built, a furniture factory had existed on the site. Maria squinted at the faded newspaper article on the screen. *Six Dead in Factory Fire*. Again, she wondered just how many had died on that land. She'd bet that there had always been tragedy and loss of life on the site. It was cursed. Maybe it had been built over a graveyard, and whatever hunted the hallways of the Parker thought its boat had come in with so many people to terrify and dreams to infiltrate. But what was it—this spirit or demon?

Maria searched online for sleep demons. Pages came up about sleep paralysis and how people thought they had scary creatures sitting on their chests, making them unable to move or scream for help. This was more than a bad dream, though; she knew that one hundred percent. Whatever it was, it thrived on hurting people in their sleep. It had hurt her and made her more poorly than she'd ever been before, infecting her so badly it could have killed her. It must be strong to have that kind of power.

Maria closed the laptop and placed it on the coffee table. Technically she should go to the station and try to find information regarding the crimes in '79 herself. But it would take a lot of time, a lot of sifting through files. She didn't have that kind of time to spare. She'd wasted almost forty-eight hours feeling crappy and now she was better, she was keen to get on with the hunt. But she couldn't shake the unsettled fear that had taken root inside her. It felt as if something big and scary was coming, and she had no way of stopping it. Because she had no idea what that *thing* was.

TWENTY-FOUR

He was running a fever. He knew by how damp his skin felt and the way his polo shirt stuck to his skin. Four murders. The voice had told him it had to be four. That would feed its soul and release it from inside the walls of this hotel. Then he would be free, too. He'd killed three already. If he could just find one more victim, he could leave this place and never come back. He wouldn't look back.

He didn't want to know who—or what—the voice belonged to. It scared him too much. He knew it was evil, he knew it was old, probably ancient. He didn't care what it would do if it got free, as long as it left him alone. The feet were an offering; he'd figured that much out. The dark spirit—whatever it was—worshipped female feet and saw them as some kind of prized possession.

The smell in the water tower was bad. He sat cross-legged, rocking back and forth, trying to quell the sickness that was threatening to erupt. He didn't need the smell of hot vomit in here as well as the stench of rotting flesh. Cupping a hand to his mouth, he stood up and rushed out of the small door, letting go the remains of his breakfast and the black coffee all over the asphalt of the rooftop.

"Hey, are you okay?"

The voice shocked him so much he almost lost his grip on the handrail and fell down the steel ladder that led up to the water tower. He looked around for the person the voice belonged to. The woman from yesterday stood by the edge of the rooftop, a cigarette in one hand and a look of genuine concern on her face. Lifting his sleeve, he wiped his mouth and wished he had a bottle of water to rinse it with.

He nodded. "Yeah, ate something that disagreed with me and now I'm paying the price."

She grimaced. "Ugh, I hate it when you pay for takeout and they give you food poisoning. As if the cost of their shitty door dash wasn't bad enough, they have to make you sick, too. Maybe you should call it a day. I'm pretty sure whatever you're doing up there will wait. I mean, the water supply to my apartment is fine. It's working okay."

He liked her, and it made him sad that they could never be more than two people who pass the time of day. She was attractive. He would have asked her out on a date if he was the old version of himself, before this blackness took over his life. Now it could never be and that made him feel even worse. He closed the tower's door and snapped the padlock he'd put through the handle into place. Then he climbed down the ladder. His legs felt like they belonged to someone else, and his hands struggled to grip the metal rungs. When his boots touched the rooftop, he let out a sigh of relief.

"Do you come up here much? Until yesterday I've never seen you before."

She shrugged. "Until the day before yesterday, I'd quit these." She flicked her cigarette on the floor, standing on it with her boot.

"What made you start again?"

"Finding those girls' bodies. I can't get them out of my head. I keep thinking about who they were, what they were like and what the fuck they were doing here. I mean, this place isn't the kind of place two teenagers should be hanging around in. What brought them here and why did some sick fuck do that to them? He cut off their feet. It's all I can think about."

Staring at her, he struggled to contain the shame and horror he felt about what he'd done. But as much as he liked her, she was becoming a pain in his ass and pretty soon she might try to look in the tower. Then it would all be over. He took a step towards her, peering over the ledge. If he pushed her, the cops would be crawling all over this place. They might put her death down as a suicide, but what if they checked out the tower? He turned away, sidestepping to put some distance between them, in case the voice took over and he did push her without thinking. He didn't trust himself.

"That's sick. Why would someone do that?"

"There are some sick people in this world. Probably got a mommy complex and blames her for everything. Talking about sick, you do look bad. You should call it a day and go home, lie on the couch and watch TV all evening. Just don't order any more takeout." She laughed and he grinned at her.

"Yeah, I think you're right. I'll tell them I'm going home, thanks. That's good advice." He was a little annoyed that she'd assumed he hadn't cooked for himself, but he let it slide. It was easier to go along with whatever she said.

She shrugged. "I'm great at giving good advice, I just suck at everything else." She stepped away from the edge and headed towards the emergency exit. "Nice seeing you again. Take it easy."

And then she was gone, back into the stairwell. He wondered if she realized how close she'd come to dying. In the blink of his eye, she could have been freefalling to the sidewalk at the speed of light. Painting those dull grey slabs in splashes of vivid red blood as she bled out on the cold, unforgiving floor outside the Parker.

TWENTY-FIVE

Frankie dropped Maria off at her apartment. Now he was waiting for Betsy to finish a call and meet him at Breads Bakery across the street. He sipped a cappuccino and ate a muffin to keep him going.

He was worried about Maria. She looked ill and wouldn't accept his help. He knew she wouldn't go back to the ER; he was lucky she'd agreed to go yesterday. But he was concerned. They had a killer to find before he struck again, and they kept getting sidetracked. He saw Betsy's outline pass the window. She was wearing a striking emerald-green dress and long black coat with a sparkling Chanel brooch pinned to it. She was older than he was; he could see strands of silver running through her red pinned hair. She was the most attractive, out-of-his-league broad he'd ever had the balls to ask out for coffee.

"Frankie, it's good to see you again."

He stood up. "It is, and it's even better to see you. What can I get you?"

"I would love a peppermint hot chocolate, heavy on the whipped cream and chocolate flakes, because I need a pick me up."

"No problem. Do you want a pastry or muffin?"

She shook her head. "The drink will be just fine. Thank you."

He sauntered to the counter with a grin on his face. When he glanced back, she was staring down at her phone, tapping out a message with her two thumbs. He never got how anyone could do that. It took him forever to send a message using his one finger. He placed the drink on the table in front of her.

"Thanks, Frankie. How is it going with the case—any leads?"

"We've narrowed down a list of hotel employees who had access to that room, but we haven't caught up with them all yet. Maria got sick, really sick, and I've been worried about her."

Betsy stirred her drink then took a sip. The cream stuck to her top lip, and she lifted a finger to wipe it off, then sucked it clean. Frankie almost died there and then as he tried not to watch her every move.

"What kind of sick? Is she okay?"

He shrugged. "To be honest, I don't know. She hurt her shoulder in her sleep, and it's got all infected." He looked around the room and lowered his voice. "This is going to sound crazy, but she said she was having a nightmare and some shadow guy stabbed her in the dream. She woke up with a deep wound on her shoulder and she hasn't been well since."

Frankie watched her face to see her reaction. She nodded. "Wow, that sounds terrible. Is there anything I can do to help her?"

"Gee, I hope not, doc, she's still breathing."

Betsy gave a look of mock horror and then she threw back her head and laughed so loud everyone else in the café turned to stare. Frankie grinned. He loved the sound of a woman's laughter. Christy, his ex, didn't see the funny side very often.

"Frankie, that's bad. And please, if we're going to be civilized and meet for coffee out of work then call me Betsy."

"Okay, Betsy it is. I don't think there is anything you can do. She's had a tetanus shot, antibiotics, everything she needs."

"Good, but I mean it, Frankie. I've always had a soft spot for the pair of you and I will do anything I can to help. So, these leads... do you think they're going to prove worthwhile?"

Frankie nodded. "One of those guys had access to the room and was in contact with those girls. How else could they have got inside without checking in as guests? We're going to speak to them all later on, see if any of them start to sweat. I've got someone running background checks on them."

"Good. I thought I was hardened to the horrors of this city. I've seen terrible things, like yourself, but those girls... it really hit home. I want you to find the guy, and find me their feet so they can be put to rest without them missing."

She took hold of his hand. He marveled at how soft her skin felt, how warm her touch was, and he didn't want her to let go. For some reason, he'd imagined that Betsy Conner would feel as cold as the dead bodies she dealt with, and he was pleasantly surprised.

"I promise you I will do my best to find them."

She let go, sat back in her chair, and sipped her drink before answering. "There was no DNA on the bodies. This guy knows his stuff. He wore gloves, he used a bone saw to remove the feet. The cuts were clean, no hesitation marks whatsoever, which tells me he's used to this kind of thing. You should check out the hotel employees' backgrounds, see if any of them have ever worked in a butcher, or in a kitchen. Somewhere they'd cut up dead animals, a slaughterhouse maybe. They could even be medically trained, but I'd have to question that because it's a bit of a leap to go from working in a hospital to a hotel."

"Not if you got kicked out of med school, it isn't. That's a good call. We'll take a deep dive into their employment histories. Where are you off to after this?" He was thinking she had a court appearance, an appointment maybe.

"Wholefoods. My pantry and fridge are sadly lacking in supplies that aren't moldy, out of date or shriveled up."

"You dress that way to go food shopping?"

He didn't mean it as an insult. He just tried to picture Christy getting all dressed up like this. Even Maria didn't do fancy unless she was going to some fancy place.

"I think you don't mean that how it sounded, and yes, in case you wondered, when I'm not in scrubs, I like to dress this way. Look at you, in a fancy suit and soft leather loafers that I know are not good for tramping around crime scenes in, yet you sacrifice those expensive shoes for the sake of, what? Looking good, looking smart?"

He squirmed a little, realizing he'd opened a can of worms and had probably insulted her. "I wear them because they make me feel good."

She held out her palms. "My point entirely. I dress this way because why the hell not? I like to feel smart. Don't get me wrong. Some days I lounge around in my pjs. Some days I work sixteen-hour days in scrubs, and on others I get to wear a nicely cut dress and shoes. But I don't need to explain myself. I'm only doing it because I like you." She winked at him, and he felt his cheeks burn.

"I'm sorry. That was a dumb ass thing for me to say. It's none of my business and Maria would have slapped me for being so stupid."

She smiled at him. "You and Maria have a special bond. It's nice and it's also probably good that she can guide you when you need it most. After I've stunned Wholefoods with my appearance, I'm going home to cook something nutritious and delicious. Let's face it, with the number of burgers and fries I've eaten this week, my cholesterol level is dangerously high. If you finish interviewing the staff and don't get tied up, then you're welcome to join me for supper. Don't feel as if you have to say yes. I won't be offended, Frankie. I'm a big girl but I thought it would be nice to maybe have a bottle of wine and take some time out of our busy lives to relax for a little while."

Frankie thought that his face might crack from the pressure of the smile that had broken out on it. He nodded furiously. "I'd love that, thank you."

She took out her phone and he told her his number. She sent him a message with her address on. "Don't give that to anyone else. I don't let many people come to my place. It's my sanctuary away from all of this and I don't let anyone in lightly. I'm making an exception for you, Frankie, because you wear loafers to crime scenes, and I like you."

He laughed. "Flattery will get you everywhere. I like you, too, Betsy. How do you feel about dancing?"

She tilted her head. "Ass twerking? Miley Cyrus or Lizzo's hot dance moves?"

"No, although I do enjoy watching Lizzo doing her stuff, that's for sure. I mean ballroom dancing."

"Like *Dancing with the Stars*? Are you telling me you can dance? Like really move your feet in time to the music?"

"I'm not saying I'm good, but I can move. I've been going to classes for almost a year now. I could take you dancing some-time." He didn't tell her the reason he'd been going to class was to impress his soon to be ex-wife.

"You are full of surprises. I would like that."

He couldn't stop smiling. "And I would like to have supper with you."

"It's a date. I have to run; I have an appointment before I go food shopping."

"You're bad."

"I am, but it served you right. Call me when you're on the way and don't worry about what time it is, I know the score. I know things might crop up and if you can't get there at all don't worry about that, too. Just let me know so I can eat your food before going to bed and sulking." She winked at him, turned and walked away. As she did so, Frankie thought that Doctor Betsy Conner might have taken a piece of his tough, old heart with her. He wanted her to keep it because he had never felt this way about a woman, not for a very long time. The exception was Maria but only when he was drunk and feeling sorry for himself.

TWENTY-SIX

Maria couldn't believe how much better she felt. The fever had gone, along with the burning sensation that made her shoulder feel as if it was on fire.

She called Frankie. "Where are you?"

"The morgue."

"Did the doc call you down there?"

He paused. "Sort of."

Maria was getting annoyed at how evasive he was being. She wasn't used to it.

"Well, she did, or she didn't, which one is it?"

"She didn't. I went to ask her out for coffee."

They both paused. Maria wished he could see the smile on her face. "Amazing. Did she have anything for us? Like a fistful of that murdering asshole's hair matching a DNA profile on the database?"

"That was a no. She said the bodies were clean. The perp must have had prior experience of using a bone saw because there were no hesitation marks. Jeez, it gives me the creeps just thinking about it. I've asked Jerome to run in-depth background checks on the names Rick gave us, but I think we need to see their personnel records and take a closer look at what their employment history was before working for the hotel."

"Okay, well, the good news is I'm ready to get back to it. I feel much better."

"You do? That's great, I'm glad to hear it. I'm on my way back for you. Maybe we can get some work done now."

She let that one slide, not in the mood to argue with him. "See you soon."

Frankie drove to the first address on the list Rick had sent over. Buzz lived in Queens; in fact, all the employees except one lived there, who lived in the Bronx. Which made it easier for them. Two of them even lived in the same block of apartments, which Frankie was parked outside of. It was quiet on the street, and he peered over the steering wheel. "You think the car is safe if we leave it?"

"Frankie, there's nobody around to do anything to the car. Besides, what are you worried about? It's not your car."

"Paperwork, that's what. We have enough on our plates without having to file a damage report." He jumped out. "Come on, don't waste time."

Maria followed him, biting her tongue. He'd wasted a couple of hours hanging around for Betsy this afternoon. They walked up three floors to where Buzz lived and hammered on the door. It was silent inside. To make sure, Maria pressed an ear to the door. "Nobody home."

"Let's try Travis. He's one of the contractors, not permanent staff."

"And what floor is he on?"

"Eight."

"Yeah, figured he would be. Are we taking the elevator?" She walked to the wall and pressed the button. Nothing happened. It didn't even light up. "I guess not." They trudged up another five flights before reaching the eighth. Maria sniffed the air and grimaced. "It smells bad up here, not like downstairs."

Frankie, who was mopping his brow, leaned against the wall to catch his breath. "Smells like there's a decomp somewhere up here. It stinks. Wonder where it's coming from? That's all we need, some long-dead neighbor who nobody spoke to and didn't bother to check when they hadn't seen them for weeks."

Maria pointed to a swarm of blowflies further down. "Follow the bugs, they always know the way."

"Aw, come on, Miller, you're not going to do this now, are you? We're busy enough. Call it in and let a patrol take care of it."

"What number does Travis live at? Actually, don't even tell me. I bet it's the one with the swarm of bugs crawling all over it."

"Thirteen—and why would it be his?"

Maria didn't even flinch. Why wouldn't it be number thirteen? As they walked closer, Frankie muttered, "I can't believe his neighbors haven't thought this is wrong. If my next door smelled like this, I'd call the cops."

"I have a bad feeling about this."

"Oh, you do? Well, you know what, I do, too, and now we're here, we can't walk away." He unholstered his gun. Maria did the same while also taking out her walkie-talkie and asking for backup.

"What's the plan?" asked Frankie. He cupped his free hand across his nose.

"We wait for the cops to come put the door through, or I could just knock. Maybe Travis isn't so good at housekeeping and we're getting carried away."

She strode towards the door, waving the cloud of bugs away, and used the butt of her gun to hammer on the door. There was no noise from inside. Bending, she lifted the flap and staggered backwards, the smell of decomposition was so bad. Frankie watched as she struggled to contain the vomit threatening to erupt all over her feet. Sirens in the street below signaled the arrival of their backup and Maria was glad. They could put the door through and deal with whatever was inside, unless they found an obvious homicide.

"You think he's the guy? How many bodies do you reckon he has inside his apartment? I'm saying two, because if he is the guy, he likes them in twos."

Maria shook her head. "What if it's Travis who's dead in there and we have this all wrong?"

"If it's him, I'll buy you breakfast."

"Fine."

Pounding footsteps echoed around the stairwell and Maria smiled at him. "They're quicker than we were."

"Anyone is quicker than us."

"Detectives, what have you got?"

Two female cops appeared at the top of the stairs. "Smells like a decomp in number thirteen."

The redhead who spoke first nodded. "Smells bad."

The blonde, who looked far too young to be out patrolling the streets of Queens, sniffed the air and pulled a face. "Did you knock? Has anyone seen whoever lives there recently?"

"No, we called you guys because we're homicide detectives and know a dead body when we smell one." Maria tried not to sound sarcastic, but it came out wrong and she saw the blonde's lips straighten into a tight line.

"If you're homicide, then isn't this your deal?"

"It will be when you get access for us."

The redhead held up a hand. "It's fine, we'll sort it." She walked up to the door and pushed the handle down with her elbow. The door swung open, and Frankie turned to Maria who shrugged. "Oops, my bad."

He glared at her while trying his hardest to suppress his

smile. The redhead tugged on a pair of gloves. "You want me to go in first?"

Maria shook her head. "It's okay, I can. I just need you guys here to deal with the scene. We're on a tight schedule and it's getting worse by the minute. Can somebody get me a photo ID of the occupant, Travis Massey?"

Frankie was on the phone to the Parker, asking for Rick urgently. Maria stepped inside the small apartment. The front door opened into the lounge area and on the couch was the body of a man. His throat was a gaping, black wound. A river of dried blood ran down the familiar uniform of the Parker staff. Maria stared down at the green and blue marbling on his face. His skin had started to slip, making his eyeballs droop down onto his cheeks. It was grotesque. There was a lanyard around his neck, and she looked for something to turn it around with, so she could see if this was Travis. Taking hold of a pen, she flicked the lanyard the other way and saw that it was empty. His ID badge was missing. She glanced at Frankie.

"I think the perp followed Travis home, killed him for his ID. Probably took his spare uniform, too. We need to find out who the hell is pretending to be Travis Massey and where he is now."

The blonde walked in, took one look at the corpse, and rushed out onto the walkway. The sound of her retching filled the apartment. The redhead shrugged. "Second week, first homicide."

Frankie smiled at her. "Ah, the first sucks, even if she is a little too big for her boots. What's your name?"

"Angie and she's Marty."

"Well, Angie, as much as we'd like to run this, as you may be able to tell we're from the 6th Precinct, so this is not our jurisdiction. You're going to have to call one of Queen's finest detectives down to deal. We will, however, help out and give statements. We're looking for the perp who murdered the two

teenagers at the Parker a couple of days ago and that's our prior-
ity. Looking at the state of Travis, I have to say that I think he
could also be a victim of the same perp, and you can pass that
on. He contracts out of the Parker, but his ID is missing. When
you get assigned a detective, give them my card and tell them to
call me." He fished a card out of his suit jacket.

"What, you're gonna just leave us here like this?"

"There's nothing we can do. If we deal with it—which our
lieutenant won't let us do anyway—we're going to waste time by
not chasing down the guy who did this. He's long gone and, if
I'm not mistaken, likely hanging around near the Parker."

Maria didn't speak. He was doing a good enough job of
passing the case off.

"You take care, Angie. You know the drill—don't let anyone
in until the detective gets here, and give them my card."

Frankie walked out of the apartment into the fresh air and
Maria followed. Marty didn't look too hot. She was bent double,
sucking in deep breaths. But the air out here was just as fetid as
the air inside. Frankie patted her on the back. "It gets better, the
more you see. Best thing you can do is get back inside and take a
good look at the decedent. Try and stay in there, acclimatize
yourself to the smells, the state of the body. Trust me, it's hard,
but you will get used to it."

She glared at him, and he sauntered off. Maria followed
behind. When they were out of hearing distance, she whispered, "What's going on?"

"I figured we need to get our asses to the Parker and speak
to Rick, see who the hell he's been letting in with Travis's ID.
We can find out when he last turned in for work, get the camera
footage and ID him before anything gets wiped off the system.
We have an actual lead, Maria, and I'm not letting it get away.
It's the closest we've got. How long do you reckon Travis has
been dead?"

"Five, maybe seven days."

"Uh huh, I agree until the M.E. tells us different."

Maria smiled. "Let's go to the Parker. Maybe you're right and he is hiding there in plain sight. We could've walked straight past him."

"You're not scared to go back?"

"I don't particularly want to, but we need to, so let's do this."

Maria was afraid to admit to Frankie that she was terrified of the hotel, that she'd rather do anything than go back up to the thirteenth floor. She knew something dark and dangerous was hiding out there. She'd almost got so sick she could have died because of what it did to her. Maybe it was time to face her fears and get rid of the darkness inside the Parker for good, so the guests and residents could live their lives in the light, not cast under the shadow of death.

TWENTY-SEVEN

Before they even got back to the car, Maria's cell vibrated. She looked down at a message from Harrison.

Cherry, aka Veronica Harry, is alive, living in a retirement home. Sunny Days in Queens. That's all my researchers could find. See you later x

"Well, I'll be damned."

"What?"

"Harrison sent this." She showed her cell to him, and he nodded.

"Is that supposed to mean something? 'Cause I'm struggling."

"In the seventies, the victim who survived was a street worker called Cherry. She's still alive. I think we should do a detour and go speak to her."

"Why? She's not going to remember much if she's in a retirement home."

"Whoever is doing this... we've assumed they are copying the killer from the seventies. But that guy was never caught. What if it is *the* guy?"

"Hang on. This is familiar. Didn't we have this situation on West 10th Street?"

"Similar, I'll admit, but we knew for definite that perp was dead so it couldn't be him."

"Even if he was in his twenties back in the seventies, that would make him in his seventies now."

"It's possible. Look, I don't think we can ignore this. There's something bad in the Parker, especially inside that room. Cherry might be able to help."

Frankie sighed. "What's the zip code?"

Sunny Days was a sprawling, white stucco building behind high, steel gates and a six-foot wall. It looked out of place in this area, but it had probably been here long before the buildings around it. A security guard at the entrance came to speak to them. Maria rolled down the window. At the same time, she held out her badge.

"Hi, we need to talk to one of the residents, can you let us in?"

He nodded. "Is it official?"

"Yes."

"Oh, that's too bad, but yeah, I'll open the gates for you."

Back in his cabin, he must have pressed a button, because the gates began to slowly open.

Frankie shuddered. "I hate these kind of places, gated communities where they sell you a dream of living your retirement safe and happy. How the hell can you be happy, having to get permission to leave the place?"

"I think they serve their purpose. Maybe some of the residents have Alzheimer's and it's for their own safety."

"I still think they look too much like a mental institution."

It was a warm afternoon, yet there was nobody around to enjoy it. There were wooden chairs under the porches of the house, but they were all vacant, which Maria found a little creepy. She pressed the intercom at the entrance and the doors clicked. Nobody wanted to know who they were or what they were doing. Frankie arched an eyebrow.

"Too trusting or did the guard warn them?"

"The guard warned them."

"Good afternoon, detectives. I'm Melody, the nurse in charge this afternoon. How can I be of assistance?"

"Is it possible to speak to Veronica Harry?"

The woman in the pink scrubs smiled. "You can. I need you to sign yourselves in, though, and do you have some identification?"

She pointed to the visitor's book. Maria leaned down to write both of their names in it while Frankie showed her his badge.

"Is it bad news? Do we need to get a member of the team to come and sit in?"

"No, nothing like that. We're looking into a cold case from the seventies and hoped that Veronica might be able to help."

"For real? Wow, that's interesting. I don't know how much she'll be able to help but she still has all of her faculties up here." She tapped the side of her temple. "Unlike a lot of the patients. She probably wouldn't be here if it wasn't for her disability, but it's a struggle to manage at the best of times, and especially when you're getting older. I'll show you to her room, then I'll go grab her. She's just in the rec room doing chair yoga."

Melody led them along a hallway that smelled of cabbage. It wasn't pleasant but compared to where they'd come from, it was like an expensive bottle of perfume. Maria would take cooked cabbage over decomposition every time.

"This is the private visiting room. We use this for stuff that the other residents shouldn't be listening to. They gossip worse than a gaggle of nuns after confession time."

A smile played across Maria's lips. That was a new one, even for her. They went into a room, with beige walls and a matching beige couch, coffee table and cushions. Melody shut the door, and Frankie caught Maria's eye, and they both laughed. They soon shut up when the door opened, and Melody pushed a woman in a wheelchair inside. Veronica looked the pair of them up and down with shrewd eyes. Maria smiled and held out her hand.

"Detectives Maria Miller and Frankie Conroy from the 6th Precinct."

Veronica had a firm grip, and she shook Maria's hand up and down several times. "Veronica Harry. What can I help you with?"

The woman, although old and frail, still bore traces of the beauty that had never left her, despite the hard life she must have lived working the streets. Maria didn't look down at her feet; she wouldn't make a point of it. Frankie, on the other hand, was staring at the stump where the elderly woman's right foot should have been, and Maria wanted to elbow him in the gut.

"You can leave us alone, Melody. I'm sure I'll be fine. Unless I'm about to be arrested for something and if that's the case then that's fine, too. It would be the most exciting thing to happen to me in years."

Melody grinned. "Push the bell if you need me."

"I will, honey."

She left them staring at each other. Veronica finally broke the silence.

"Do you want to put me out of my misery and tell me what's going on?"

Frankie took a seat opposite her. "Yes, sorry. This might be upsetting for you, but we have some questions regarding the night you lost your foot."

Veronica's eyes almost popped out of her skull. Her mouth opened wide and then she shut it again. "I didn't lose my foot; I knew exactly where it was until Arnie cut it off. It wasn't as if I lost a purse or my sweater. The damn thing was attached to my body before it was chopped off, taken by force, removed without my consent. But it wasn't lost, detective, so let's get that clear."

Frankie's cheeks burned, and Maria was glad it was him who'd broken the ice, even if it was in the worst way possible. "That's what Frankie was trying to say, only he's not so good at finding the right words. You'll have to forgive him for being stupid. He means well."

Frankie glared at Maria, and she smiled sweetly back. Veronica, on the other hand, laughed, her eyes sparkling with mischief. "I'm sorry, I didn't mean to be so cruel. I've always had a dark sense of humor."

Frankie was still glaring at Maria, giving her his best *Can you believe this broad?* expression. Maria liked her already. They knew all too well that dark humor was what got them through some of the toughest cases of their lives. Why wouldn't Veronica use it in the same way? Maria grinned at her.

"Veronica, there has been a double murder at the Parker and both girls had their feet removed. They were only teenagers. I'm trying to figure out what is going on. If it's a copycat or if it could be the same killer."

Tears glistened in Veronica's eyes, pain, too, at the long-buried memories Maria had just brought back. She shook her head. "No, it can't be."

"Unfortunately, it's true. I tried to research what happened to you in the press but there wasn't anything apart from a little side bar."

"Stanley, what a guy. He took care of me really good when he didn't need to. Took care of medical expenses, then gave me a job in the hotel with good benefits. At a point where I could've died and probably should have died, he turned my life around, and I'll never forget his kindness. The hotel had just spent a fortune on remodeling—big publicity—and they didn't want this being front page news. So, they paid the press to keep it quiet. Besides, it wasn't that great a news story. A hooker got her foot cut off by a pissed-off John. Nobody really cared. Stanley put me on the payroll when I was taken to hospital. He saved my life that day in more ways than one. He's a good guy. He never wanted anything in return and that is a very rare thing. How is he? I hope he's not still working his ass off in that dump."

Maria shook her head. "He's retired and loving life in an ocean-view apartment on Coney Island."

Veronica nodded and smiled. "Ah, that makes my old heart happy. He deserves a life away from that place. Once it gets its dirty little claws in you, it's hard to tear away. I only knew Arnie for a few hours. We met in the basement bar. He was nice to me; we had a good time, and he didn't even want sex, which I should have known was a bit odd. I mean, you get the odd trick who only wants to talk 'cause nobody listens, but they are rare. Arnie wanted company and somebody to talk to and I wasn't about to complain. But he also seemed torn. I could tell by the way he kept playing with his wedding band that he wasn't sure about what he wanted to do. I didn't care one way or the other. All I cared about back then was making enough to pay the rent and keep my alcohol levels topped up. It's funny. I never touched a drop after I came out of hospital. It didn't have the same appeal."

"Did Arnie tell you about his wife, anything personal at all?"

"Nothing, never mentioned her. We went up to his room, emptied the mini bar and I fell asleep. I broke all the rules of the street that night—and boy, did I pay for it. I was too trusting. I just really liked him and didn't want it to end. He made me feel safe. I never in a million years expected what happened to happen. I've never really spoken about it since. I didn't even tell the cops back then the whole story because it was kind of hard to believe. But I've dwelled on it a lot over the years, and I know I'm not crazy. I saw what I saw."

"What did you see?" Maria leaned forward, wondering what the hell she was about to tell them.

"I saw him disappear right in front of my eyes. One minute he was there, the next... I thought maybe at the time it was because of whatever drugs he'd slipped in my drink, or the shock was making me hallucinate. But deep down I knew it wasn't either of those things." She paused, taking a moment, and closed her eyes. Maria could tell she was back there in room 1303, reliving the pain and horror of that night. She didn't rush her. Eventually, Veronica stared right into her eyes.

"I saw him get pulled into the drywall. One moment he was standing facing it, the next this black shadow thing came out of the wall and took hold of him, dragging him into it. There was this loud popping sound. He opened his mouth to scream but no sound came out. I don't know what took hold of him, but it was strong. After only a couple of seconds, he was gone. All that was left of him was a bloodied handprint on the wall. That's when I started screaming. The pain was so bad I can't remember much after that. Apart from Stanley. I remember him telling me his name as he held my hand waiting for the para-medics. I'm not senile; you can ask the nurses. I don't ever want to talk about this again. I'm only telling you now because you said that two girls have been murdered in that room and I'm scared it's starting all over again."

Maria stared at Veronica, not sure what to say, as she tried to process what she'd just revealed. "Arnie—he was never seen again?"

Veronica shook her head. "The police searched the entire hotel; I asked them if there might be secret passages behind the wall and they thought I was nuts."

"What do you think happened to him?"

"Are you taking me seriously?"

Maria nodded. "We've worked some cases that are hard to give a rational explanation to. It's what we do."

"I think he's trapped there, in the Parker. Something evil lives in that hotel. I don't know if any other people have gone missing, but if they have, then I imagine they're trapped, too. Then again, maybe that shadow thing wasn't evil at all? If it hadn't taken him, I would have died, so maybe it saved me. Gee, I've never thought about it that way before, and now I'm conflicted."

Maria shook her head. "I don't think it's a good thing, whatever it is. I think it craves people's pain and misery. You said yourself that you and Arnie were getting on well. He might not have been able to control himself when he hurt you. The shadow probably thrives off that kind of thing. I believe it's some kind of sleep demon that preys on guests at their most vulnerable. It thrives off their nightmares, slipping into their dreams as if it belongs there, taking control of them. It makes them sick, too, infects them with evil."

A horrible thought occurred to Maria: if she hadn't been cleansed by Father Anthony, would she have turned evil and begun hurting people? She couldn't say for sure, but it was a possibility.

"All I know is that place scares the crap out of me. Just thinking about it... How are you going to stop the shadow creature? Do you know who killed those girls? Can you be certain the killer is still around and hasn't been sucked into the drywall like Arnie was?"

Maria couldn't. She'd come here for answers and now she had even more questions.

Frankie, who hadn't uttered a word, broke the silence. "That's a hard tale to tell, Veronica. Thank you for sharing it with us."

She shrugged. "What else could I do? It's been so long. I could pretend it never happened and keep my head buried firmly in the sand, or I could try to help. Although I don't know how useful any of that is to you. Maybe you could break through the drywall in that room and see if there is anything behind it."

"Like Arnie's body?"

Veronica nodded. "He can't be alive, can he? Not after all this time. How do you survive that long without food or water? How do you survive living your life trapped in the shadows?"

Maria reached out and patted Veronica's hand. "Thank you. Would you consider going back there?"

"No, I have no desire to go back to the Parker. Stanley told me I never had to go back to the thirteenth floor, and he kept his word. I worked in a back office for a time. I literally hobbled in, sat at a desk for eight hours then hobbled back out again. When I retired, I swore to myself I'd never set foot in that place again. I don't know what use I'd be if I did. I'm too old to be fighting evil shadows and I certainly don't want to end up getting sucked into the wall to be stuck with the guy who chopped my foot off for all eternity. I'm sorry about those girls, but I can't do it."

"I understand. Thank you for being so candid with us and for trusting us with your story."

Maria stood up and Frankie followed her. "Take care, detectives. I hope you can figure out what the hell is going on in that place, I really do, because it's time somebody put a stop to it."

They walked out in silence, both processing what they'd been told, trying to figure out where they went from there. At that moment, Maria had never felt so torn and confused.

TWENTY-EIGHT

The nearer Frankie got to the Parker, the harder Maria's stomach clenched. What was happening inside the hotel's walls? And how long it had been happening for?

"We need to see the blueprint, see if there are any hidden crawl spaces somebody could live in."

"You think that this Arnie guy was a magician? That he convinced Veronica he'd disappeared but really went into a hidden crawl space and has been living there all this time. For real?"

"I don't know what I'm thinking but we can't ignore the possibility."

"Geez, I find that hard to swallow. I'd rather believe something dragged him into the wall. We know stuff like that exists, we've seen it with our own eyes. You said yourself you got stabbed in a nightmare about the place and you were really sick. How did you get better? Because a couple of hours ago you looked terrible."

"Missy called Father Anthony. He came and blessed me. Poured a bottle of holy water over my wound and said a prayer."

"You're shitting me?"

"Not even one tiny bit."

"Then you know something bad is going down in that place. Why are you saying otherwise?"

"I'm scared. I don't want to go back in there, but I know that we have to. We need to find out who has been impersonating Travis Massey before they kill again. Because I think that they will, now they're on a downward spiral. We're the only ones who can stop him. Or…" She paused. "Or whatever took Arnie, maybe it's taken him."

Frankie shook his head. "I can't wait to hand my notice in. I don't think I can take this anymore. It's not good for my heart."

Maria reached out and gently clasped his hand. "I don't think I can either, so let's finish this and tell Addison we're through chasing demons. Deal?"

"Deal."

Inside, the hotel foyer was gloomy. Maria didn't look up at the windows from out on the sidewalk, for fear of what she might see. She'd managed to cheat the fate the woman in blue had dealt her and she wasn't risking it happening again.

The sound of arguing crossed the marbled floor. Maria saw the two sisters from the day of the murder having a face-off with one another. Rick came running out of his office, calling out, "Ladies, ladies, let's take a moment." It looked like neither Jo nor Angie was willing to take a minute; instead, they turned to face him.

Jo spoke first. "What is your problem, Rickie?"

Maria hated domestic arguments. They were beating the crap out of each other one minute, the next they were beating the crap out of you for trying to intervene. Nevertheless, she walked in their direction, much to Frankie's disgust.

"My problem is that you are causing a scene in the foyer.

There are guests around. Can you ladies not take it up to your apartment?"

"And where's the fun in that? Nobody could hear us up there, Rickie," said Jo.

"You want people to hear you bickering like a pair of old broads?" asked Frankie incredulously, and everyone turned to him.

"Well, yeah, that's the whole point. We are trying a social experiment, and it looks like you lost, Angie. Nobody truly cares what goes on in this hotel except for him." She pointed at Rickie.

Maria looked around at the people milling about and saw that it was true. Nobody was paying the slightest bit of attention to the sisters, despite the scene they'd caused.

Angie turned to Rickie. "We're sorry, please accept our apologies."

Rick waved a hand in their direction, his eyes blank. He shook his head and strode back towards the desk.

"He's mad with us," whispered Jo.

"So what? Let him be."

Maria found the two women both fascinating and annoying as hell. "What kind of experiment?"

Jo pointed at her sister. "She thinks that the longer a person stops here, the more invisible they become. Nobody ever looks at us when we come and go. Look at what happened on the thirteenth floor. Some guy managed to murder two girls, and nobody saw shit. Angie thinks there's some kind of supernatural force at play in here."

"Doing what?"

"Suppressing people. Sucking the life out of them. Feeding off them."

Maria wondered if her day could get any more bizarre. She also agreed with Angie's theory, but wasn't going to admit that to them. They still had to live here; at least she could go home and escape—or could she?

Angie glared at Jo. "Come on, I need coffee. We'll catch you later, detective." And they walked away, leaving Maria feeling confused.

Frankie whispered in her ear, "Those two are cuckoo."

Maria didn't agree—they had clearly picked up on something, and she believed them. She watched the women walk towards the exit for a moment, before running to catch up. "It's not true. I noticed you the other day."

Angie smiled at her. "But until the other day, you hadn't set foot inside this place, had you? It hadn't got its dirty fingers into you yet. If you want some advice, keep away from here and don't come back, unless you really have to. I feel as if we're trapped here whether we want to be or not. That's our lot."

Jo and Angie carried on walking, leaving Maria staring after them. Veronica had said something similar. None of them knew that this place had done more than put its claws into her—it had almost killed her.

She reached for the simple gold cross she wore around her neck, a present from Missy and Emilia. Each time she touched it, she felt a wave of love so strong from her friends, and she knew she could face whatever came her way, because she was protected. She could do this... she *would* do this, no matter what.

Maria walked into Rick's office to see him pulling up the building's blueprint for Frankie on the desktop computer.

"We probably have got the originals someplace, but I couldn't tell you where."

Frankie peered over his shoulder. "That's okay, these are better than nothing."

Maria joined them. "Can you focus on the thirteenth floor?"

"Not really. I can only think of one person who might know where the original plans are."

"Stanley," said Maria, and Rickie nodded. "One minute, I'll call him."

Maria walked out and rang the number she'd saved for him.

"Hello?"

"Hi, it's Detective Maria Miller. I came to see you the other day."

"How are you? Is everything okay?"

"Not really. I'm with Rick and we're trying to find the plans for the hotel. Would you know where the originals are kept?"

"They used to be kept in the safe, but I think they got moved when the hotel had to shut."

"Do you know where to?"

"Head office, I would think. I don't know why they didn't leave them behind. Rickie should be able to get a scan of them up on his computer though. They digitalized everything and, if you ask me, ruined the whole goddamn world at the same time."

"Yeah, he's got the scan up, but we want to focus on the thirteenth. Tell me, did you ever come across secret passageways in the hotel? Or do you know if there are crawl spaces that run between the rooms, big enough for a person to hide in?"

"You spoke to Veronica, huh?"

"We did. She spoke highly of you."

"She's a good woman who got dealt a rough hand in life. I was glad that I could help her. How is she? Where is she? Can you tell me that?"

Maria hadn't got the information from the police database, so she decided to share it with him. "Queens, in a retirement home called Sunny Days."

"Thank you. I might go pay her a visit."

"I think she'd like that."

"In answer to your question about the crawl space, the hotel is full of them. Ask maintenance, they are your best bet. In fact, I wouldn't be surprised if they didn't have a copy of the blueprint. Those guys probably use it to keep the place up and running. I don't think there are crawl spaces near room 1303, though. It's smack bang in the middle of two other rooms."

"What about the window wall with the balcony? Which wall did Arnie leave the bloodied handprint on?"

"The wall next to the balcony. I'll be damned. There could be space there, I suppose."

"Thanks, Stanley." Maria hung up and went back to see the zoomed-in plans of room 1303. There *was* a gap between the balcony and the bathroom—a space that looked big enough to fit a person inside. Maria smiled at Rickie. "Where are maintenance? Would they happen to have a sledgehammer?"

"I can't let you go in and smash the room to pieces. I just can't."

"That room is a mess. It's going to need a whole lot more than a coat of paint to make it right. I don't see what difference a few holes in the drywall will make."

Rick let out a groan. "You two are killing me. I've got a wife and I need this job to pay my bills... You're gonna get me sacked." He stared at them for a moment, then nodded. "You're not giving me a choice, are you? Maintenance is in the basement; I can take you down there."

Maria realized then that they hadn't broken the news about Travis to Rick yet. "How well do you know Travis Massey?"

"I don't, not really. He's kind of a quiet guy, keeps to himself, always wears a New York Yankees baseball cap."

"I have some bad news for you. We attended his home address earlier and found him deceased."

"*What*? How did that happen?"

"He was murdered. What I need to know is, had he been into work the last couple of days?"

Rick ran a hand through his hair. He stood up and began pacing up and down his office. "Yes, he was here yesterday. I haven't seen him today."

"Was he here the day of the murders?"

He squeezed his eyes shut for a moment. "I think so. I saw him briefly getting in the service elevator, then things got screwed up. It's hard to keep track of the staff. I deal with maintenance occasionally but not very often."

"Can you get me any video footage of Travis?"

Rick sat down at the bank of CCTV monitors and typed at the keyboard. "I can't remember the exact time I saw him on the day the girls' bodies were found."

"Did you speak to him?"

"No, I waved at him from behind the desk. He lifted a hand and waved back as he was getting into the service elevator."

Maria looked at Frankie. Rickie had probably waved at the killer and not Travis. She was going to have to be the one to tell him. Rick got the footage up from the morning of the murders. The time stamp said 07.01. There weren't many guests around, but they spotted a couple of maids and a guy dressed in black combats, desert boots and a New York Yankees cap. He kept his head down as he crossed the floor from the main entrance, lifting a hand to wave at Rickie who was out of this shot.

"Do staff always come in through the main entrance?"

"No, we don't encourage that. They have a staff entrance around the back alley where they can smoke, shoot the shit, and have a break without the guests seeing them."

"Then why didn't Travis use it that day?"

He shrugged. "I can't say. I didn't think much of it. The maids try to keep out of the way, but maintenance are more hands-on and have to fix blown lightbulbs, broken doors, that kind of thing."

"But did he have a reason to come in through the front door on the day of the murders?"

He shook his head. "Nope, there were no jobs listed here for that day. There was a problem with the water tower but I'm not sure who sorted that one out."

"That wasn't Travis. It can't have been: he's been dead more than three days." Frankie said it without thinking and Maria felt her whole insides cringe at his insensitivity.

Rickie turned and stared at him. "Pardon me? Travis has been dead for how long? That's ridiculous, he's been in work. I saw him yesterday before I left for a meeting."

"Did you speak to him yesterday?"

"No."

Maria gave Frankie a look, and he shut up. She turned to Rickie. "I'm so sorry for your loss— were you close?"

Rickie sat down, his legs seeming no longer able to carry his weight as he buried his head in his hands. "What the fuck is happening with this place? Are you sure it was him?"

Maria thought about the missing ID badge from his lanyard. "We're not a hundred percent sure until he's been identified by his next of kin, but it was his apartment, and he was wearing the same uniform the bogus Travis had on."

"What does this mean?"

"That Travis was killed by the perp who stole his clothes and ID. Somehow, the killer—posing as Travis—arranged to meet the girls at room 1303. They went inside thinking they were going to have a look at the famous murder room. Instead, they became the next victims. He knows this hotel. He has probably been staking it out, stalking the staff, the guests, biding his time until everything fell into place. How easy would it be for someone to wander around the floors without anyone getting suspicious?"

"I'd say anybody could do it, as long as they kept their heads down and didn't cause a fuss. People are coming and going all day long. It's impossible to keep track of everyone. Certain guests and long-term residents stick in your mind, especially those two annoying sisters." He looked down, sadly. "I bet Stanley would have known that guy wasn't Travis. He knew everyone."

It occurred to Maria that the perp could be in the hotel at that very moment. "Did you see Travis come in today?"

A look of panic crossed Rickie's face. "I... no... I don't think so. Oh crap, he could be in here doing anything. Let me get security on it."

Her eyebrow raised. "You have security? Where are they?"

"We have Isaac in the basement when he's on shift, but he's better on the cameras down there than I am up here. I only have basic knowledge and monitor the foyer; he has access to all the floors."

Rick led them to the staff elevator before pausing. He waved Shanice over. "If you see Travis around, can you let me know? Have you seen him today?"

"Who's Travis?"

"The electrical contractor."

"Oh, that guy. He's weird, never speaks. Yeah, I'll tell him you're looking for him."

"*No*, I don't want to worry him. Just let me know where he's heading, and I'll take it from there."

She nodded. "Sure thing, Rickie." Guests were already queuing at the desk, and she headed back to deal with them.

"Nicely played," muttered Frankie.

Maria smiled. "You handled that well; we don't want to cause a panic, especially if he's not even here. If we do see him in the building somewhere, we'll call in SWAT to come take him down."

Rickie's complexion was the color of gone-off milk. He looked like he was going to throw up. "I can't imagine the implications of a SWAT team running riot through the hotel." There were beads of perspiration forming on his brow and he took out a tissue to blot his forehead.

Frankie replied, "They won't run riot. That's the whole point of the SWAT team. If we think we can take him without anybody getting hurt, then we'll deal with him. If he's going to pose a problem in a public place, we have to call for backup. It's the rules."

They found Isaac downstairs, sitting in a small booth surrounded by monitors. He grinned at Rickie when he saw him.

"Good afternoon, boss. What can I do for you?"

"Isaac, these detectives are looking for Travis Massey. Have you seen him around?"

He shook his head. "Not for a few days. Let me look at the book." He let himself out of the booth and picked a book up off the table. "This is the workmen's register; they have to log in and out so we can keep an eye on the hours and where they are working." He scrolled through the pages, turning back six days where he found Travis's signature. "He hasn't been in for six days. I figured he was on another job maybe or took some time off."

Maria felt a wave of grief for the man who'd gone home from his shift only to be murdered for his ID badge, with nobody to report him missing.

Rickie sat down on a chair next to the table. "Then who the fuck has been pretending to be him?"

Isaac looked at Rickie then Maria. "Does somebody want to tell me what's going on?"

A group of giggling maids exited the elevator. They took one look at Rickie's face and the noise ceased instantly. They hurried along the corridor through a door that said *Female Changing*.

Maria explained the situation to Isaac, who was beginning to get twitchy. "It's not your fault, but has anybody signed in you didn't recognize?"

He shook his head. "People, workers, are coming and going all day long. I pride myself on knowing all the permanent staff, not so much the contractors. But there hasn't been anyone using this entrance to get into the hotel that I haven't seen before."

"Then he's been using the front entrance upstairs. He must have realized he'd get caught if he tried to come in this way. Isaac, can you go through the footage and make a copy of any contractor who uses the main doors? Would you know if he's come in here today that way? It's urgent—can you go through the footage now?"

He nodded and they followed him into the cramped cubicle, watching as he rewound the camera footage to midnight. "We'll take it from here, in case he's moving around when the day staff aren't on."

They watched as Isaac fast forwarded through the footage, right up until Frankie and Maria walked through the doors. "It doesn't look like he's here right now. I take it that's a good thing?"

Maria smiled weakly. "Yeah, but we're going to need you to keep a close eye on the entrance."

He peered at Rickie over the rim of his gold-framed spectacles. "Boss, I can only do what I can do. I can't watch the foyer *and* go through the footage. My eyes aren't so good at the best of times. What do you want me to do?"

It was Frankie who answered. "Find us the last sighting of him. We need you to go through the footage until you see him and then call us so we can come and take a look. We need to find this guy ASAP. Rickie, you're going to have to monitor the entrance and do the same."

He nodded. "I can do that. Isaac, you keep on searching and let me know when you get a hit."

"What about bag checks?"

"Not today. This is more important than a couple of bottles of handwash."

They left Isaac in his booth and went back upstairs. "Rickie, we need access to room 1303. Is there some kind of key that could get us into most rooms in the hotel if we had to?"

"I'll give you a master key card. They open everything, but I can't have you going into guests' rooms or apartments if they're occupied."

"We wouldn't dream of it unless it was to save a life."

He pulled a card wallet from his pocket and handed Maria a white and gold card. "This is mine, take care of it and don't abuse it. Better still, don't lose it either."

She smiled at him. "We won't. Thanks for your help, Rickie."

He arched an eyebrow at her. "Now I'm Rickie. You're dropping the formal Rick?"

"You have become a trusted ally. Now you're Rickie."

He smiled back. "I'd like to think that's a compliment, but I'd rather that none of this had happened and we'd never met."

Frankie laughed. "Can't blame you for that, but we do our best under the circumstances."

Rickie grinned at them. "You go find that sick son of a bitch before he hurts anyone else, and I'll owe you for the rest of my life."

"And the crawl space?"

"If you need a hand to knock the drywall out, I'll get hold of Buzz to bring you a sledgehammer. I guess we're in it up to our necks now whether we want to be or not."

TWENTY-NINE

Emilia paced up and down the apartment, and Missy couldn't take it anymore.

"What's wrong with you, dear? There's a track running through my best Persian rug."

Emilia looked pale. If Missy was asked to describe her, she would say that she looked like an old woman today, and it was the first time since they'd been reunited that she'd thought of her best friend and partner that way. They were old, there was no disputing that. And Missy made jokes about their age all the time. But clearly something niggled away inside Emilia, making her feel worried and uncomfortable.

"I can't settle."

"That I can see. I don't need my sixth sense to tell me you're unsettled. But why are you feeling this way?"

Missy knew exactly what she was going to say. She wanted to get up and leave the apartment before the words were said out loud and couldn't be taken back. Instead, she waited for Emilia to gather the right words.

"Maria needs our help; she cannot deal with that thing stalking the halls of the Parker by herself."

Missy's throat felt dry and scratchy. "What do you suggest?"

"You're not going to like this one little bit, but I think we should get a cab and go find Father Anthony then go to the hotel, the three of us, ready to assist Maria."

"You're right. I don't like it."

Emilia came to sit next to her. She gently took hold of Missy's hand. "I won't ask you to do this. I don't want to see you in danger. But I can't shake this feeling that we have to go there."

Missy pulled her close, wrapping her arms around Emilia's frail shoulders. "You know I'll always be there for you."

Emilia kissed Missy's cheek. "I'm sorry, I'm asking a lot, but I feel as if Maria is like the daughter we were never blessed with, and I can't stand by and let her deal with whatever monster tried to kill her on her own. I want to help and protect her. We won't get too involved, but I would like to take a look at the place, to get a feel for it, so we can formulate a plan of attack. That won't be too bad, will it? We can manage that, surely, without getting into any trouble."

Missy lifted her hand and kissed it. "If you want to do that, then I do, too. Come on, you old softie. Let's go and find that handsome young priest and drag him into some more trouble. If he doesn't request a transfer after this, then he's made of stronger stuff than I ever imagined."

Emilia smiled and it melted Missy's heart. She loved this woman more than she ever thought she could love a person. She was her life, and she would follow her to the deepest depths of hell if she asked her to.

THIRTY

Mina was bored. She wanted a cigarette but had told herself one pack of smokes to calm her nerves and that was it. Allowing herself that luxury, she'd thoroughly enjoyed every single one. She hadn't smoked for years, but the horror of finding those girls had shocked her. She couldn't get the brutal image of their bodies out of her mind. So, she had gone to the kiosk on the corner of the street and bought a pack, telling herself she needed them, deserved them.

She made herself an espresso and stared at the packet on the side containing her last cigarette. She could go up to the rooftop and see if that cute guy was up there. What the hell was he doing in that water tower anyway? Maybe he went up there to hide so he didn't have to work his ass off all day. That's what she would do if she had a manual job. Find herself a hiding place where she could sit on her phone scrolling through Instagram or watching funny memes.

Pulling on her thick jumper, she picked up the cigarette packet. She was so upset by what had happened she'd even thought of calling her ex-husband Joey to see if he could come see her. That was a very bad idea because Joey was an asshole. He always had been, probably always would be. How she'd managed to stay married to him for ten years was a constant source of wonder to her. He'd been funny and kind when they met, and she supposed the sex had been great. They'd screwed in some strange places. She blushed whenever the images of her straddling him in an elevator somewhere without a care in the world came into her head. For a moment she felt sad that it had ended so badly. They both worked too hard in order to pay for the apartment they lived in and had stopped making each other laugh. She should have known that was the beginning of the end.

Laughter had kept them going for a while; when things stopped being funny, so had everything else. It was like a competition to see who could be the meanest to one another. She'd said some pretty nasty stuff to him, most of it she hadn't even meant. She just liked hurting him, and slowly he'd stopped loving her. One day, when she'd headed to his office to drop a file off, she'd heard his laughter and it had made her smile. Then she caught a glimpse of him with his hands all over some woman's ass. She had gone straight home and packed her stuff. She was many things, but stupid wasn't one of them. Mina had got in a cab and headed straight to the Parker, intending for it to be a temporary stop. That was six months ago, and she was still here. Joey had found out where she was and come to see her. She had expected him to beg her to come home; he didn't. He brought the rest of her stuff and told her he was moving Chantelle in with him—the girl with the ass he'd had his hands all over.

In the hallway, Mina passed the two detectives who'd spoken to her the day she found the bodies, and she wondered what they were doing up here on the tenth floor.

"Hey, are you lost or something?"

Maria smiled. "Mina, how are you doing?"

She shrugged and flashed the cigarette packet at her. "Not so great. I can't stop thinking about them, those poor girls. Can't get the images out of my mind. I don't know how you guys do what you do day in and day out."

"Somebody has to. It's not easy to push it to one side. We still struggle after years of being cops. Maybe you could talk to someone about it, might help."

"What, like a therapist? I'd rather stick hot pins in my eyes, thanks. What are you doing up here?"

"Looking for maintenance."

"Oh, sorry. I haven't seen anyone today. Rickie should be able to call them for you. Have you spoken to him?"

"We did. It's okay, I'm sure we'll find someone. Hey, while I have you, have you ever seen the woman in blue up here?"

Mina had heard all the tales about the ghostly figure of the woman who'd cut off her own hand and now haunted the place, but she had enough problems of her own without worrying about a depressed ghost. She shook her head, thinking it was a weird thing to hear a cop ask a question like that.

"Can't say I have, sorry."

Mina walked away, heading towards the stairwell. She carried on towards the rooftop stairs. She didn't care what they were doing as long as it didn't involve her. She wouldn't do their job for a million bucks. She couldn't handle the death. The thought of dying made her shudder so violently her whole body shook. That was the reason she gave up smoking a couple of years ago. She wasn't risking getting lung cancer. Mina made up her mind. She would savor every minute of this cigarette then that was it, no more.

The late afternoon sun warmed the roof and felt good against her skin. Mina wasn't supposed to be up here. A sign on the door said *No guests or residents on the roof except in the case of an emergency.* For her, it was an emergency. This was a mental health emergency. And besides, she'd checked. A camera looked onto the stairs, but it was broken. Someone had taped the lens over, so security weren't watching her. She might even bring herself a chair up, so she could sit and enjoy the fresh air.

She stared over at the narrow ladder which led up to the water tower. She wondered if the guy was in there now, hiding from work. She could share a cigarette with him, shoot the shit for an hour, maybe ask him out. She was tired of being lonely. Before she could chicken out, she found herself walking towards the ladder. Mina opened her mouth to shout a greeting, then quickly closed it again. He'd been pretty secretive yesterday when she'd asked what he was doing in there. Maybe surprising him would be better, then he'd have to let her in.

Gripping the rings of the ladder, she climbed up, not looking down. The metal was cool to her touch. She hoped she wasn't going to fall and break her neck. How ironic that would be. Woman scared of dying killed herself by climbing a ladder she had no business climbing. As she reached the top, she noticed the chain and padlock hanging loose. That was good, hopefully he was inside. She tugged the door open, and the stench hit her full in the face, like someone had smacked her with a hammer. Her stomach contracted as her mouth filled with saliva. Cupping a hand over her mouth and nose, she tried not to throw up. It smelled like the garbage cans of a butcher shop that had been left outside for days baking in the heat. Had the guy died in here?

Having left her phone in her apartment, Mina lit her zippo and looked around. The small space was hardly big enough for anyone to walk into. She turned slowly. At least there wasn't a body on the floor. She looked up at a beam of wood that ran above the doorway, unable to understand what the growing buzzing noise was. That's when she saw a black teeming cloud of movement—and realized they were blowflies. Mina let out a screech. The flies took off into the air and she saw what they'd been crawling all over. On the ledge were two purple and black rotting feet.

Mina pushed herself out of the door, completely forgetting there was only the tiniest ledge of a walkway and missing the ladder completely. Her arms waved as she free-fell through the air. She hit the rooftop with a loud thud. Her head took the brunt of the fall. Blood seeped from the deep wound on her head. All her fears had happened at once.

Mina groaned. Somebody was dragging her, and every single jolt sent shockwaves through her head and down into her shoulders. She blinked, trying to open her eyes, but they were sticky, and her eyelids felt as if they'd been glued shut.

"Everything hurts. Am I in hospital? I can't see." Her voice was a hoarse whisper.

Mina smelled body odor tinged with something bad, something rotting, and then she remembered the feet in the water tower. She opened her mouth to scream, and a rough, callused hand clamped across her mouth, cutting her off.

"Shut up. if you make a fuss, I'll break your neck right here."

She knew she was no longer outside on the roof. She was inside, could feel the rough, threadbare carpet burning her bare feet. Where were her shoes? She'd been wearing them when she climbed that ladder. Had they fallen off when she took a dive towards the roof? She tried to clear her head. The blackness was threatening to take her down into it.

He dropped her in a heap on the floor. She heard the stair door being opened. She felt him bend down close to her and thought she might throw up. That would serve him right. Why wasn't he getting her medical help? She tried not to think about the rotting feet. Then she was being moved again. The faint smell of burning still lingered in the air and she began to panic.

He was taking her to the room... the one where she'd found the girls.

This time she did scream, but it was cut off by a punch to her jaw so hard it knocked her head back and loosened a crown. She could taste metallic, vile blood pouring from her mouth. Before she could do anything, he hit her again.

And for the second time she lost consciousness.

THIRTY-ONE

They'd checked every floor but the thirteenth. Frankie hadn't questioned Maria when she'd gone straight up to nine then the tenth. Now, as the elevator doors slid open on the thirteenth, Maria held her breath. Her phone vibrated in her pocket, making her let out a small screech. She ignored it. She focused on not losing the guts to deal with this floor. The ringing stopped only to start again immediately.

"You better answer that."

"I don't want to." She couldn't say how or why, but she had a bad feeling that whoever was calling wasn't going to tell her anything good.

"Maria, answer the damn phone, it's just gonna keep on vibrating."

She didn't know the number, but she recognized the breathy voice on the other end. "Maria, it's Father Anthony. Can you speak?"

"Yes, what's wrong?"

"It's Emilia, she's collapsed. We were coming to see you, but she wanted to go to the Parker first, insisted that we come here, and she only stepped into the foyer..."

"Are you still there?"

"Yes, paramedics are on the way, but she doesn't look good."

"I'm at the Parker now. I'm coming down."

The panicked look on her face told Frankie something was very wrong. "Got to go downstairs, Emilia collapsed."

"What! Is she here?"

Maria pressed the call button and the doors slid open. A flock of birds seemed to flap their wings frantically inside her chest, making it difficult to breathe. She wouldn't know what to do if the outcome was bad. Poor Missy. She and Emilia were so close and so happy after years of being alone. It seemed as if time had slowed down completely as she repeatedly jabbed her finger at the G button.

When the doors finally opened, she ran towards the entrance. Rickie, Anthony and Missy were all crouched on the floor. Paramedics ran in at the same time as she crossed the marble floor to get to her friends. Anthony was helping Missy up, giving the paramedics room to work on the elderly woman. Breathless, Maria looked down at Emilia—her pale face and slack jaw—and she knew then that it would be a miracle if she made it.

She lunged for Missy and pulled her into a tight hug, wrapping her arms around her. She turned her slightly so she couldn't see what the medics were doing to Emilia as they ripped open bags to canulate her. Anthony had his hands clasped together, holding a set of rosary beads. His lips moved silently as he prayed for Emilia. Maria felt herself rocking Missy gently, the way her mum used to do with her when she was upset as a kid. Maria wanted to scream. This place was cursed. It was nothing but bad luck. And Emilia wouldn't have set foot in the Parker if it hadn't been for her. This was Maria's fault. Once again, she'd dragged her two close friends into something they had no business being a part of. The guilt was like a bullet charging toward her heart.

When Emilia was stabilized enough to be transported to the ER, Missy insisted on going with her.

"I'll be right there, I promise." Maria reached out and stroked Missy's cheek and the woman clamped her hand to her face, kissing Maria's fingers.

"No, you will not. You will sort this place out. Something evil stalks through it, taking what it wants, and it has to stop; you two need to stop it. Emilia was looking up at something on the top floor when we arrived—something had caught her attention completely. She couldn't tear her eyes away from the tenth floor."

The sickness in the pit of Maria's stomach was hard to contain. She wanted to throw up, wanted to walk out of there and say screw it. She wasn't being a part of this anymore. It was time to let somebody else take over this case, because fear was turning to anger.

As Missy headed out of the door, she turned back to her. "Anger is good. Don't let it know that you're scared. I'll call you with an update as soon as I have one. This isn't your fault, Maria. You didn't ask either of us to come here. We came because we are too damn nosy for our own good."

Anthony shook his head. "We came because we wanted to help."

Missy nodded, then she was out of the doors onto the street and being helped into the back of the ambulance by a medic. Maria thought her heart was going to break. She couldn't stand it. The thought of losing either Missy or Emilia was crippling. They were closer than her own family. She loved them both dearly, like the grandparents she'd never met.

Hot tears pricked at her eyes, and she turned away so Frankie, Rickie and Anthony wouldn't see them. She wasn't a weak person, but this was almost too much to bear. They gave her a minute.

When she was ready to face them, Maria turned around.

"What are we doing? We need to regroup and come up with a plan. We didn't even get to the thirteenth floor. I mean, we literally stepped out of the elevator and you rang, then we stepped back inside."

Father Anthony nodded. "If I didn't know any better, I'd say that it caused Emilia to collapse to divert your attention away from the thirteenth floor."

"Then it's scared. And if it's scared, then it's intelligent, whatever the hell it is," muttered Frankie, who looked almost as distraught as she did. He loved Missy and Emilia, too.

Rickie looked around at the guests who were still loitering. "My office, I'll get some coffees brought in whilst we have a think, or if you'd prefer something stronger…?"

Frankie, who usually wasn't one to turn down a stiff drink, replied, "Coffee would be great and some pastries, too, or cookies, whatever you can get your hands on."

Maria led the way as Rickie picked up the front desk phone to dial the restaurant. Within minutes, a waiter walked in carrying a tray with four coffees, a sugar shaker and a plate of mouth-watering cakes that even Maria couldn't take her eyes off.

"Thank you, Johnny."

Johnny nodded. "You're welcome, sir. Is there anything else I can get you?"

"No, thank you, that will be all."

Nobody spoke until he'd backed out of the room, closing the door behind him. Frankie reached over and picked up an XL-sized macaron. Rickie pointed at the cakes. "You've all had a shock; sugar will help you process that and concentrate on what happens next."

Maria felt like screaming in his face that a fancy cake wasn't going to solve anything but managed to stop herself. Instead, she picked up a vanilla cupcake with swirls of frosting. Her hands shook. She couldn't get the image of Emilia out of her mind. She nibbled on the cake and sipped the coffee. Father Anthony didn't accept a cake, but gladly took a cup.

Rickie didn't touch the food either, and instead leaned against the wall. "What are we going to do? I wish I had the number for the Ghostbusters. I loved the film when I was a kid. I'd gladly pay them to come and get rid of whatever the hell is haunting the thirteenth floor."

Maria closed her eyes. Opening them again, she looked at Rickie. "You don't need them. You have us and we've done stuff like this before. Well, not quite like this, but similar. We need to go and see what the hell is behind the wall in room 1303." She knew fine well what they might find behind the drywall—some kind of clue that Arnie had entered through it and never come out. Maybe even his skeleton. It being stuck there might be the cause of everything that had happened these past few days.

Rickie took out a walkie-talkie. "Buzz, can you come to my office ASAP with a sledgehammer, please?"

Father Anthony nodded. "Is this to fight the ghosts with? Because I'm not sure it's going to work."

Maria realized he'd need to be brought up to speed about what was happening. "Do you have any of that holy Evian water?"

He laughed then stopped when he realized she was being serious. "No, sorry, I don't. I didn't know this was going to turn into this. I thought I was just coming for a peek with the ladies to get a handle on what was going down. I didn't foresee any of this, and it's kind of taken me by surprise. Although, I can bless any water and it will be holy."

"Would it be strong enough to fight a dark entity?"

"Maria, it's blessed water. It should be good enough to fight Satan himself."

Maria wondered what level of darkness they were about to face—demon or human—but she didn't say it out loud. She didn't want to scare anyone. They were all waiting for her to answer when a sharp knock on the door made all four of them yell out with fear. An older guy with a headful of white hair walked in, swinging the biggest sledgehammer Maria had ever seen.

"Jesus, you made me crap myself, all that shrieking. What the hell is going on?" He noticed Anthony and crossed himself. "Father, I'm sorry, I didn't see you sitting there."

Anthony lifted his hand. "It's okay. Buzz, is it?"

Buzz nodded. "After the astronaut, not the cartoon spaceman."

"Well, Buzz, I guess you drew the short straw." Buzz turned to look at Rickie who shrugged. "We need to take down a wall in room 1303. Can you do it, or should we?"

Buzz looked at each one of them in turn. "I want to say you can do it yourselves because I get the feeling that there's something going on here that is way beyond my pay scale. But I'm not a slacker and never have been, so, Rickie, you better lead the way."

"Well, I appreciate your candor, Buzz, and I'll bear it in mind. Are we done, suitably refreshed?" They all nodded at Rickie. "Good, well then, let's get this show on the road, and if I still have a job by the end of today, it will be a modern-day miracle."

Anthony grinned at him. "We're always looking for new miracles. The old ones are a little outdated."

For some reason this made Maria chuckle. "Buzz, we don't know what the heck is going on either. You're going to have to trust us on this, okay, and do what we ask. Have you been in room 1303 lately?"

"Nope, you wouldn't catch me going inside that room unless I had direct orders to."

Maria realized they hadn't mentioned Travis. "Have you seen Travis around today or yesterday?"

"The contractor?"

"Yes."

"No, he hasn't been in all week."

"Damn it. Have you seen anyone that you didn't recognize wandering around?" The words left her lips before she could stop them. Buzz watched her carefully, then he asked, "Is someone going to tell me what is really going on?"

Rickie smiled. "All in due course, Buzz. Let's go take out this wall and then we can catch up and see how you're getting on." He patted him on the back and Maria felt bad. Here was another innocent guy they were involving in something that could be life-threatening for him.

"I have to go in 1303?"

"Yes, but we're all going with you. It will be fine."

Buzz didn't look convinced, but his boss had just given him a direct order and he didn't look like the kind of guy to ignore it. Four men and one woman walked out of Rickie's office and Maria prayed all of them would survive whatever was hiding in room 1303—and walk out of it together.

THIRTY-TWO

Maria felt as if some kind of dark, ominous music should be playing in the elevator. If this was a movie, the music would be telling the audience they were about to approach something so terrible they should hide behind their hands. They exited the elevator and stood in a line, afraid to go first. It was Maria who did.

"We can't let it dominate us like this. We have to make a stand—it's now or never."

She didn't turn back to look at the others, but she knew Frankie would be right behind her. He was her partner, her wingman, the guy who had helped her figure out how to deal with the last two cases they had been involved in. She suspected that Father Anthony was close behind Frankie, because he was a good man. He wouldn't let her go into a room that was tainted with evil alone, without God's protection, and for that she was glad. Father Anthony had known what he was getting into when he joined the priesthood. He may not have actually believed that evil things walked the earth among the living, but he was primed and prepped in case he came across them. So, he, in his own way, had signed up to fight the forces of evil.

She felt bad about Rickie and Buzz. Neither of them had signed up for this. Maria and Frankie had, when Addison had asked them to run the strange cases department, for a ten grand a year incentive. They'd both jumped at the chance. Now, though, Maria would hand back every single penny to be back on homicide, answering straightforward calls.

The hallway was dark, much darker than it had ever been before. Maria saw that most of the bulbs were out. It reminded her so much of West 10th St—the darkness, the demon living in the wall, the missing body parts—and it took her a split second to finally get it. They must be connected. How many places could a beast like that hide? How many of them were there? What if when James Carter had opened that portal in the old brownstone in 1952, he'd been more powerful than he had ever imagined. Was that why his sister Emilia had such a strong reaction to walking inside the Parker? Had she felt it, too?

Maria glanced at Father Anthony. He didn't have a bible in his hands or the holy water they'd been joking about. "Stop." The guys all did as she asked. "Father Anthony, where is your bible and holy water?"

"No bible. I told you, I didn't know this quick peep at the hotel was going to end this way, so I left it behind." He tugged a half-drunk bottle of water out of his pocket. "I have this, though."

Frankie arched an eyebrow at him. "Gee, I feel so much better knowing you have a half-drunk bottle of water. Everything is good now, praise the Lord."

It was Anthony's turn to arch his eyebrow. "I did a silent blessing on it in the lift. It can do the job if we need it to. Not everything has to be all singing and dancing. The biggest miracles happen in the smallest of ways. All you need is your faith; that is your armor. God's love and light is your weapon."

Buzz nodded. "Amen to that, Father. I go to church every Sunday, have done since I was a child. I'm not even going to ask what you're hoping to find or fight in that room. I'm just here for the laughs."

Maria chuckled and it felt good. She didn't know whether to tell them about her new theory because she knew it sounded insane. But then who knew a shadow could chase you through your dreams and stab you? Make you so sick you could have died? "Before we go inside, can we join hands and pray because I have a feeling this is bigger than any of us can imagine?"

Rickie looked as if he'd rather brand himself with a hot poker, but he reluctantly took hold of Buzz and Frankie's hands, and they formed a small circle. He whispered, "If a guest comes out now, they're going to think we're some kind of cult."

Maria smiled. "Don't worry about the living. It's the dead we have to protect ourselves from." And she clasped hold of Father Anthony's and Buzz's other hand, wondering where that line had come from. It sounded like a Missy quote.

They listened as Father Anthony said a prayer of protection over them all and they all whispered, "Amen." One of the two remaining light bulbs flickered then went out. Father Anthony broke the circle first. "Well, it knows we're here. Should we get this show on the road?"

A few more steps and they were outside room 1303. Maria didn't know if the others were the same, but she felt as if it was the end of days. She hoped they weren't going to set in motion a chain of events that would change everything for the worse. Frankie looked around and nodded. "Who is doing the honors?"

Buzz stepped forward. "I'm the maintenance guy. I fix the problems around here. I ain't afraid of no ghost either."

He reached up and tore down the yellow crime scene tape; crumpling it up into a ball, he dropped it on the floor. Maria could have hugged him. Father Anthony crossed himself as Buzz pressed the key card to the electronic pad and the door clicked. He pushed the door open; the room was darker than she remembered. Father Anthony pressed the switch, letting light illuminate the empty space. Maria had been half hoping that the killer was hiding out in here, had gravitated towards this room like James had towards the attic in West 10th. She'd hoped there would be a scuffle and the perp would be cuffed and taken away from the hotel forever.

Buzz turned to Rickie. "Which wall do we have a problem with, boss?"

Rickie pointed to the wall next to the windows. In a few steps, Buzz was swinging the sledgehammer at the drywall. The guy was strong because it went straight through and left a hole the size of a football. He kept swinging, as Father Anthony kept praying, until there was a sizeable hole that could fit a person's head and shoulders through. Maria used the flashlight app on her phone to light it up; neither she nor Frankie had thought to bring a proper one with them. She stepped up to the wall and looked into the space and jumped. "Oh, God, I was right."

Frankie stepped next to her. "What do you see?"

She gave him her phone. "There's a skeleton in there."

Rickie's face crumpled. "You have got to be shitting me. How the fuck did it get in there?"

Frankie handed the phone to Buzz, who took one look and said, "Holy crap—sorry, Father."

Father Anthony smiled at him, as Buzz offered him the light to take a look. But he shook his head. "I'm happy to take your word for it."

Rickie paced up and down. Maria wondered how many pairs of shoes he went through in a year because the guy did a lot of pacing. "Now what?"

She looked at Frankie. "Now we have to get access to it, so Buzz, can you make that hole bigger? When we can reach it, I want Father Anthony to go in and bless it. Can you give the last rites to someone who was a bad person?"

"It won't hurt to try."

She turned to Rickie. "Then we are going to have to call in forensics."

"How are you going to explain finding this?"

"Buzz was doing some maintenance and stumbled across it."

Maria was convinced that once they removed Arnie's body from the room, everything would be okay. Maybe it wasn't anything more than a simple haunting? She was happy to go with that theory. Get his body taken to the morgue and even though he was a terrible person, he'd still get a proper burial and put an end to his reign of terror over the Parker.

THIRTY-THREE

Frankie kicked at the wall. Maria kept staring at the twin beds where the girls' bodies had lain. She had a niggling feeling inside her that something wasn't right. This was all too easy, too straightforward. She had expected a bubbling torrent of horror to greet them, yet this wasn't anything like that. Maybe it wasn't always that way. Maybe God had got there first and had lent a helping hand. But who'd killed the girls? Where was the perp? What the hell was he doing right now?

Rickie's walkie burst into life. "Boss, it's Isaac. I found something on the cameras you might want to come and see."

"I'll be down shortly."

Maria looked at Frankie who was now covered in plaster dust. "I'll go take a look with Rickie. Are you guys okay up here?"

He nodded. "Up to now. I'll call you if I need you back here."

Rickie released a sigh, and she followed him out of the door. "I'm going to shut this room off for good. As long as I'm working here, it is not getting let out to guests. I'm not having my staff

going in there either. As soon as you're done, I'm taking it out of
commission, and I don't give a damn what management say."

She smiled at him. "You're a good boss, you know that,
right?"

He shrugged. "I try to be. Stanley's boots were hard to fill,
you know, and it's taken years for anyone to even talk to me as if
I'm a real person and not a robot."

"Stanley's boots might have been hard to fill, but I think that
yours are just as big."

"Thank you, that means a lot."

They got in the elevator, and he turned to her. "I thought it
was going to be really bad, you know? I was expecting a scene
out of *The Exorcist*, that one of us would get possessed and start
puking green peas everywhere."

Maria laughed, but she wouldn't have done if she'd noticed
the shift in his eye color as they changed from a clear turquoise
blue to obsidian black while he stared at his reflection in the
mirrored wall. A small smile played across his lips and his
tongue poked at the corner of his mouth, causing a thin line of
saliva to fall from his bottom lip. He quickly blotted it with his
sleeve, as the doors opened on Isaac who was there waiting for
them.

"You need to see this, boss, there's some guy I've never seen
before going up and down to the roof. I don't know how I
missed him, but he's been in and out for a couple of days before
the camera up there stopped working."

Maria felt the same spark of hope ignite inside her chest
that she had whenever they got a good lead on a case. She knew
that this was what they'd been praying for. They went into the
small office where one of the monitors showed the image of the
stairwell to the roof top, paused. She could see the grainy face of
a man she didn't recognize.

"Can you take us to the first time he goes up there, please?"
He nodded and looked down at the notepad on his desk with

dates and times scribbled on it. Isaac had been busy, and she appreciated it.

"Sure thing. I can't believe I missed him. He kind of looks like Travis from a distance, but then you get a close-up and realize he's nothing like the guy. Similar height and build, but that's it, though. He's younger for a start and his eyes... they look almost black when he's staring in the camera, and he does stare into it. It's like he's not afraid of being caught at all."

Maria leaned over the desk, watching as the guy walked up to the rooftop, hands in his pockets as if he was doing exactly what he was supposed to be doing. The next clip showed him carrying what looked like a heavy bag in his arms.

"What do you suppose he has in that?" asked Rickie.

"I would have to say Michelle Carter and Dory Painter's feet."

Both Isaac and Rickie looked at her. Isaac shook his head. "For real, the dude has the nerve to walk around this place like he owns it. Kills two teenagers and takes their feet up to the roof. What the hell is he going to do with them?"

"I don't know, but I have to find out. What's up on the roof, anything of use to him?"

Isaac shrugged. "Just the water tower."

And she knew then, that was where he'd been hiding. "Have you got cameras anywhere else that have captured him on other floors?"

"Probably, but I wanted to concentrate and find every piece of footage of him going up and down."

"I'm sorry, I'm being bossy. You did good, Isaac, thank you. I'm going to need you to save all of those for me and can you print off stills?" He nodded. "Good, get as many clear ones of his face as possible." She wrote her email address down on the notepad. "Send me what you have so we don't lose anything. At some point you're going to have to send it to the official portal when I get the time to send you a link, but for now that would be awesome."

She turned to Rickie. "I need to go up to the roof."

"Is it safe? Should you not at this point be requesting that SWAT team you both talked about to come out and take him down?"

"We don't know if he's up there. He might not even be here at the moment. I just need some kind of confirmation that I'm chasing the right perp. I'll take a quick look and then decide whether they're needed or not."

He grinned at her, a real wide smile that made his face look completely different. Then he caught himself and changed to a more serious expression. Maria wondered what the hell he was finding so amusing but didn't dwell on it because she couldn't afford to waste any time.

"Come on then. Let's go take a peek and see if he's up there," said Rickie.

His attitude seemed a little different than earlier. He led the way to the elevator and let out a long, deep sigh. "Christ, I feel like I'm spending my entire day riding up and down getting nowhere fast."

"Hey, I'm sorry. I can manage myself; you can go back to work. You have been more than helpful today, and we really appreciate it."

"I wouldn't dream of it; this is work, too. I'm just saying I hope the asshole is up there so we can get rid of the skeleton and the killer all on the same day, then maybe this place can get back to some kind of normality."

As they exited onto the tenth floor, Maria caught a glimpse of blue at the opposite end of the hallway and groaned. "Did you see her?" Her voice was panicky. She didn't want to deal with this again on top of everything else.

"Who?"

"The woman in blue."

He shook his head. "Not your lucky day, is it?" He started laughing and she wondered how less than twenty minutes ago she'd begun to think he was an okay guy. She looked again, sure she could see the faintest trace of blue hovering in the air at the opposite end of the hallway. "Where's the stairwell?"

He pointed to the exact spot she had been looking at and she groaned again. "Why me?"

Rickie ignored her and strode towards the door. She hurried after him. Maybe the blue woman wasn't for her this time. Maybe it was a warning for Rickie. She glanced up at the security camera, which had tape stuck across the lens, and she hoped that CSI would get a nice print from it. She drew her gun, making Rickie flinch.

"Oh, you're taking this seriously then? I'll just hang back behind you. Would you rather I got Frankie to come give you a hand?"

"He's busy. Keep behind me, okay?"

She ran up the stairs. She didn't want to have a confrontation on the stairwell and risk the perp having the upper hand. She also didn't touch the door handle and instead used her elbow to push the bar down. She noticed it was sticky with a dark red liquid and sniffed her elbow. There was no mistaking the earthy tang of blood. But whose was it? Was he hurt and hiding up here? She really hoped so. Be even better if he'd bled to death up in that tower. She pushed the thought away. What was wrong with her? It was as if her brain couldn't think straight and was craving violence.

Pushing the door hard, it flew open and banged into the wall. She scanned the rooftop. Unless he was hiding behind something, or inside the tower, he wasn't in her immediate line of sight. The water tower was a fair distance away and she tried to calculate how far it was. How long would it take her to sprint to it? Five, ten seconds maybe. If he came out of the door, they would be sitting ducks.

"You wait here. If there's trouble, go get Frankie."

"You sure you don't want me to come with you?"

"No, I need someone ready to run for help. I left my phone with Frankie." She took off, running toward the tower and he watched her, a wistful expression on his face. A crippling pain inside Rickie's head made him clasp both hands to his ears. It was so intense it made him fall to his knees. The asphalt in front of his eyes began to blur and he felt peculiar, like he wasn't himself.

Maria was almost at the steps to the tower when she slipped in something, and her feet went out from under her. She fell to the floor with a hard thump. Rolling over and jumping up, she realized what she'd fallen into, ass first, by the smell. More blood. She cupped a hand across her mouth and begged her stomach not to bring back the coffee and cake she'd nibbled on less than an hour ago. Blood was smeared all over her butt and the rooftop. There went any valuable forensics. Not to mention her pride.

Grabbing hold of the metal handrail, she pulled herself up the stairs as fast as she could, with one hand still gripping the handle of her gun. The door swung gently in the breeze, scraping against the wooden boards. Maria reached out for it, careful not to touch the handle. She'd already ruined two lots of evidence. Grabbing a hold of the wood, she pulled it open.

"Freeze, don't move. NYPD, I'm armed and I will shoot you."

Then she lifted an arm up to cover her nostrils. It smelled as bad in here as in Travis Massey's apartment. She looked around the enclosed space. There was nowhere for him to hide unless he'd climbed into the water tank itself. She knew she was going to have to climb the narrow ladder attached to the side of it to be sure. Damn it. Why was it always so complicated? Why hadn't he been sitting in here hiding?

She had no way of seeing where the smell was emanating

from, but she could tell by the fog of blowflies hovering on a narrow ledge above her head that something dead was up there —and she knew it was going to be the teenage girls' missing feet. As she stepped closer towards the ladder and reached out for it, a heavy blow landed on the back of her head, and she let go, dazed. She tried to get her bearings, but her legs were shaky. Somebody had knocked her for six. Before she could lift the gun to shoot whoever was behind her, something hard hit her skull with a loud thud, and she blacked out.

* * *

Maria was a dead weight. As he dragged her out of the tower, he realized that getting her down the ladder was going to be a challenge. It was a good three, maybe four-foot drop. He tried to throw her over his shoulder in a clumsy fireman's lift but didn't have the strength. Instead, he rolled her to the edge and pushed her off. She hit the rooftop and didn't even stir. He wondered if he'd hit her too hard with the broken piece of metal bar he'd found by the stairwell.

Jumping down, he dragged her, careful to avoid the pool of blood that she'd already made a mess of. He had no idea where he was going. He was just following his instinct. It couldn't be long before her partner came looking, unless good old Arnie had sorted him out. He bumped her down the stairs and came out onto the tenth floor. A smudge of something blue stood in his way and he couldn't figure out what it was. He could see the color floating in the air in a haze but nothing else. Putting his head down, he carried on walking and dragged the cop behind him, until he reached a door. He hammered against it with his fist. The door opened and the guy they'd all spent hours chasing was staring at him. "You look like shit."

"I feel it. Who the hell are you and what are you doing with her?"

He pushed the man to one side, dragged Maria through the door, and closed it. There on an armchair was another woman whose face was a beaten, bloody mess. He recognized her and realized he was in Mina's apartment. "I could ask you the same question."

The man scrubbed a hand over the stubble on his chin. "I don't fucking know what I'm doing. One moment I'm doing normal stuff and the next I'm in some guy's apartment slicing his neck open so I can wear his clothes and steal his ID. What's your excuse?"

He thought about it. "You tell me."

"What's your name?"

"Arnie, or it used to be, I don't know."

"What's your name?"

The guy in Travis's clothes let out a short bark of a laugh. "I thought *my* name was Arnie. I wish I knew who this Arnie guy was because I haven't got a clue what's going on anymore."

The pair stared at each other, both trying to figure out who was telling the truth and who was full of crap. Neither of them paid attention to Maria, who was starting to regain consciousness.

THIRTY-FOUR

Frankie and Buzz stood at the entrance to the hole, looking as if they'd just survived a bomb blast. "It's all yours, Father."

Father Anthony didn't look as pleased that they were finished. "Er, should you not go in first in case of forensics?"

"There is no way in hell he got in there through anything that can be explained. These walls have never been taken out and patched up. They were as good as the day they were built; I doubt there's going to be anything of forensic value. It don't cover supernatural events in the textbooks."

The three men looked at each other. "Would it not be wise to wait for Maria to come back?"

Frankie shook his head. "She's chasing a physical lead. Can you do your thing? The quicker we put this to bed, the sooner I can go help her."

"Yes, of course." Father Anthony walked over to the scorched, soot-stained bedside table and tugged open the drawer, pulling out a water-damaged copy of the bible. Father Anthony stepped inside, and Frankie shone the light from Maria's cell on the long-dead skeleton as the priest edged his way towards it, soggy bible and half a bottle of water in his hands. Father Anthony turned to Frankie. "What's his name?"

"All we have is Arnie. We're not sure it's his real name—that was possibly David—but it's what he called himself here."

Father Anthony nodded. "Good, that's something." With a quivering hand he took the rosary beads from around his neck and dropped it over the skull onto his bony chest. There was a loud hissing sound, and the lights went out. Anthony jumped, cupping a hand over his nose at the awful stench that had come out of nowhere and filled the tiny, too-tight space he was crammed inside with the skeleton of a long-dead serial killer.

The phone died, too, leaving them all plunged into complete darkness.

"What's happening? What's that smell? Did you step on a gas main, Father?" Buzz shouted and Father Anthony let out a sigh. "Yes, I might have." He didn't sound convinced. Frankie had a bad feeling. The priest began to recite prayers.

"I commend you, my dear brother Arnie, to Almighty God, and entrust you to your Creator. May you return to him who formed you from the dust of the earth. May holy Mary, the angels—' He stopped suddenly, and the prayer was replaced with a low moan.

"Father, what's wrong?"

Every tiny hair on the back of Frankie's neck prickled, giving him gooseflesh as a blast of icy air blew out of the hole. He pulled his own cell out and held it into the space. The skeleton that had been sitting on the floor was now standing upright. One of the skeletal hands had the priest gripped by the neck, choking him.

Buzz, who was peering over Frankie's shoulder, yelled, "What the fuck in the name of our Father is happening?"

Fear had rooted Frankie's feet to the floor. But he'd only seconds to recover because the grip from those skeletal fingers had almost squeezed the life out of the priest. His face was a deep maroon as he gasped to get air into his lungs like a dying fish out of water. Frankie drew his gun, but it was pointless. There was a bang as the bottle of water Father Anthony had in his hand fell to the floor. Frankie let out a yell and dived to pick it up. Unscrewing the cap, he threw the water at the thing trying to choke Father Anthony and it let out a scream so unearthly that it made Frankie cup his hands across his ears. It released its grip and Frankie dragged Father Anthony away, towards Buzz, who helped get him out of the hole.

Then it was just Frankie and the dead thing that was gathering itself together. Frankie looked at the gun in his hands, then looked at the skeleton, aimed and fired. "Take that, you asshole. Nobody hurts a priest on my watch."

The bone exploded into hundreds of shards, and one caught Frankie underneath the eye, slicing the soft skin clean open. Blood began to pour from it. He didn't move in case the skeleton kept coming towards him, even without a skull. To his relief, it didn't. It collapsed in on itself, all the bones falling into a heap on the floor. He turned to Father Anthony. "Are you good?"

He nodded, his voice hoarse. "I never expected that."

Frankie couldn't help it. He roared with laughter, shaking his head. "Me neither."

He winced. "Look at your cheek."

Buzz rushed out of the bathroom with a wet facecloth and pressed it against the cut. "Am I tripping? Can somebody tell me that I'm tripping even though I haven't touched acid since the seventies...?"

This made Frankie laugh even harder and even Father Anthony joined in. "I wish we were tripping, Buzz, I truly do, but I just shot a freaking skeleton."

"And I almost got choked to death by one. Holy Mother of Mary. What is happening? Is it dead?"

Frankie shrugged. "It's fallen into a heap, and it has no

skull. I'm hoping it is and it's gonna stay that way. Do you want to go back and bless it some more to be sure?"

"No offence, Frankie, but if you want it blessed for a second time you can do it yourself. It didn't take too well to the Lord's words."

Once again, Frankie couldn't contain the laughter; it was so wrong, yet it felt so right. There was a flickering as the lights all came back on.

"Take that as your sign from God that we're done here," croaked Father Anthony.

"Amen to that," said Buzz who looked shell-shocked. He glanced from Frankie to the priest in amazement. "Rickie is going to be pissed about the state of this room when he comes back, and we tell him he can clear out that thing in the wall himself 'cause I do not get paid enough to deal with this crap."

Frankie picked up the sodden bible that was on the floor and threw it at the pile of old bones, expecting them to fly back at him. They didn't, and it landed with a thud. "I think we're good to get out of here. Rickie is welcome to it."

Frankie helped Father Anthony to his feet and Buzz locked the door behind them. Anthony made the sign of the cross on the door and they left to find Maria.

Frankie, Father Anthony and Buzz walked out of the service elevator, crossing the floor towards Shanice who was reading her phone at the reception desk. She took one look at them and gasped. "Get out of sight, will you? Rickie is going to go batshit crazy if he sees you three strolling through here like extras off the *Walking Dead*."

Frankie smiled at her. "Where is he?"

She shrugged. "I dunno, haven't seen him since he went off with you guys. Will you get out of here before you scare the guests?"

Buzz went to the office, knocked and opened the door. It was empty. "They could still be with Isaac in the basement."

He led them to a stairwell and Frankie was about to go down when he heard a voice call out.

"Detective Conroy," said a woman's voice. "Might I have a word?"

He turned around to see Stanley pushing a wheelchair with Veronica sitting inside. Frankie wouldn't have been more surprised to see his dead mom and pops standing there. It was just that sort of day. He walked towards them.

"What are you guys doing here?"

"I figured you might need a hand and seeing as how I haven't got a leg to stand on"—she winked at him—"Stanley kindly offered me a ride. Now, can you tell me what's going on because I haven't slept a wink since your visit? And where is your lovely colleague, Maria?"

"I'm trying to find her and, to be honest, guys, I haven't got the time at the moment."

Veronica turned to Stanley. "Park me over there. When you have got the time, I'll be waiting."

She wasn't being sarcastic this time; Frankie got the impression she was deadly serious.

"Yeah, that's cool. Honestly, you wouldn't believe what just happened in room 1303. I still can't figure it out."

"Did you find Arnie's body?"

He paused for a second, then nodded. "I can't say for sure that it's him, but he was behind the drywall that nobody has touched for decades."

"You believed me?"

"We did. I just had to fight a skeleton that somehow managed to come to life when the good priest was trying to give him the last rites."

"What happened to your cheek?"

He decided not to admit to shooting a long-dead skeleton in

the skull and blowing it apart. "I scratched it knocking through the wall."

"Can I see the room?"

He shook his head. "Not right now. I have to find Maria and then I'll see if we can get you up there for a few minutes."

"Thank you. We'll wait here for you."

Stanley stared around the foyer, his gaze falling on Frankie. "The place looks different."

Frankie smiled. Wait till he saw room 1303—that would give him something to take his mind off the renovations. He slipped through the door and ran down the stairwell to the basement, just as Buzz and Father Anthony were about to get in the elevator with Isaac.

Father Anthony waved him over. "Maria and Rickie were going up to the roof. We were just coming to tell you."

Isaac continued, "I found footage of the guy I think you're looking for—he has been going up there since a few days ago."

Frankie pushed them into the lift and Isaac pressed the number 13. He tried to control his rising panic. "How long ago was this?"

"Twenty, maybe thirty minutes ago."

Frankie felt cold fear chill his insides; thirty minutes was a lifetime when you were faced with a killer.

As soon as the elevator reached the thirteenth floor, he ran out onto the landing. For an older guy Isaac kept up, reaching the stairwell hidden at the end of the corridor. Frankie stormed up to the rooftop with his heart in his mouth.

"Maria, Maria." He cupped his hands around his mouth. He bellowed her name as he ran towards the water tower, where he saw smeared blood and a trail of bloody drag marks leading towards the door, and a discarded piece of metal piping. Blood and hair were matted on one end—the same color as Maria's. Taking out his phone he called for backup. "Send me everyone you've got—I want SWAT, I want shooters, I want the whole goddamn station here, stat."

He knew he should be pulling on rubber gloves before he touched the ladder, but he didn't care. There wasn't time. As he clambered up, the stench of decomposition filtered out of the door, making his heart skip a beat. Whatever was dead had been that way for some time, so it wasn't Maria. He charged into the water tower and breathed a sigh of relief. His best friend wasn't dead on the floor, but she was missing. And where the hell was Rickie? He realized that it might not be Maria's blood at all—it could be his.

He jogged back to the others who waited for him at the top of the stairwell. "This is a crime scene now; we need to shut this door until more cops arrive to guard it. Isaac, I need you to get on the CCTV and find me the last sighting of Maria and Rickie, like yesterday."

"I'm on it."

They hurried down the stairs to find Stanley pushing Veronica's wheelchair out of the lift. She raised a hand at Frankie. "Now I know something bad is going down. It doesn't take a genius to work that out and I can guarantee whatever it is has something to do with that shadow thing that sucked Arnie into the wall. I think you'd better take me to room 1303 to see if I can figure it out. That was the last place anyone ever saw Arnie; I think it took his body but had no use for it. It was his spirit it wanted, and I bet it's trapped in this hotel doing whatever that thing commands it to. Maybe if I can call Arnie back, we can release his soul. And then we can trap the shadow... demon... spirit... I don't know what the hell it is."

Father Anthony let out a groan. "I have no idea what is happening, but it could be worth a shot."

Frankie turned to him. "You're willing to go back inside that room?"

"I'll do what I have to."

Frankie clapped a hand on the priest's shoulder. "Good man." He didn't say it out loud, but he was terrified for Maria—and for the rest of them. Because they had no idea what they were dealing with except that it was manipulative, clever and evil.

THIRTY-FIVE

Maria could hear voices—male voices—but she couldn't see who was speaking. She had a blinding headache and could feel blood leaking from the wound on the back of her head. She managed to peer out of one eyelid to get some sense of what she was up against. She saw the blurry shape of a woman on an armchair, head drooping, hair matted with dried blood. She was moving her fingers, so she was alive. That was good.

The two of them had survived being violently attacked out on that rooftop. What Maria had to figure out was *why* they had survived, and how she was going to get them both out of here. She had no idea how long she'd been out cold for, but Frankie would be looking for her by now. He would panic when he saw the blood. Panic was good, it would spur him into action.

Maria heard sirens from the street down below. There were always sirens in the city, but there were too many in the same area for this time of day. She hoped they were going to come and rescue her from the bad guys. It was hard to concentrate, but she tried to see if she recognized the voices in the room. The betrayal was like a knife to her heart when she realized it was Rickie speaking. She had to try to slow down her breathing because it would be no use if she had a cardiac arrest now. It wouldn't help the woman in the chair—or herself.

Her mind drifted to the woman in blue. She'd seen her twice now and twice she'd almost died. The rumors were true. What a torturous way to spend all of eternity, warning people of their impending deaths. Rather than fear, Maria felt sorry for her.

"What is the plan?"

"Get them to the roof and kill them."

"I just dragged her down from the roof, I'm not dragging her back up."

The two men weren't paying attention to either of them, and Maria dared to open her eyes properly. She found herself staring at a beaten and bloodied Mina—the woman who had found the teenage girls. It had all started with her bravely putting out that fire and raising the alarm. Mina opened her eyes and stared back at her. Mina nodded once, her gaze dropping to her hands, and Maria looked down. She saw that Mina had managed to get her hands loose enough that she could slip the ropes. But would she be able to take on two guys who were not acting like themselves? She didn't know if Mina had the strength, but she sure was tough, and Maria knew she wouldn't go down without a fight.

Maria wasn't restrained. It was as if Rickie had forgotten all about her and she wondered if he thought she was already dead. Rage began to build inside her chest at the bare cheek of these men, who thought they had the right to go around smashing women's skulls in. Then the room began to get cold. The air temperature dropped so much that she saw Rickie's breath form a cloud of fog when he opened his mouth to speak.

"You served me well, but it's time to let you go."

It came out as a low, gruff, animalistic voice that made Maria's already cold skin shudder. It wasn't Rickie talking. She realized then that he'd only started acting strange since they left room 1303. The way he'd kept grinning at inappropriate moments... someone or something was inside him. Maria saw a shift in the other guy's demeanor as he looked from Rickie to Mina, to her, just before she had the chance to close her eyes. But he didn't say anything. He was too busy taking in his surroundings, as if he'd never seen the place before.

Confusion masking his face, he turned back to Rickie. "What the hell is going on? Where am I and what have you done to those women?"

Rickie walked across to the kitchen counter where there was a knife block. Maria knew what was going to happen. But the guy who'd murdered two teenage girls and attacked Mina didn't. It was as if he was coming round from a deep sleep. She saw a baseball bat propped against the wall to the left of the door and lunged for it as Rickie picked up the knife. At the same time, Mina pushed herself off the chair, picking up a glass vase filled with flowers. It all happened in slow motion. Maria managed to get to her feet. Unsteady, she didn't know how long she could stay upright for. She swung the bat as Rickie stabbed the knife. But she was too late. The blade pierced the guy's chest as Rickie plunged it in as far as he could.

The man stumbled backwards, clutching at his heart. Rickie let go of the knife as the metal bat connected with his right arm, smashing into his wrist. He issued a scream of pain. Unlike the guy with the knife protruding from his chest, he didn't make a sound as he fell backwards. Rickie turned to Maria and with his good hand grabbed her neck and began to squeeze. Everything started to turn black around the edges of her peripheral vision, except for the beautiful woman who somehow managed to glide through the apartment door. She was as clear as Mina was, and she smiled at Maria, shaking her head.

Rickie must have seen her, too, because he released his hold on Maria slightly and stared, giving Mina the chance to swing the vase at his head. With a loud crunch as the glass exploded over the back of Rickie's head, he fell to his knees. Maria felt bad. She liked the real Rickie a lot, but it didn't stop her from swinging the bat again and smashing it across the back of his head.

"Karma is a bitch," she said as he toppled forward onto the floor. Grabbing Mina by the arm, she whispered, "Can you see her?" The woman in blue shook her head and she realized then that it was just her. "Please, I don't want to die. I'm bleeding, I have the headache from hell and I'm just beginning to get my life together."

Mina stared at Maria. "Who are you talking to, me?"

"I'm here to help you, Maria. I tried to warn you, but I wasn't strong enough. I distracted him, now get out of here, before he wakes up."

"Thank you."

"I'll watch him. Rickie is a good guy but the thing inside him is using him. Go find the priest. He needs to exorcize the sleep demon before it gets free and jumps out of him."

Mina whispered, "You're freaking me out, detective. Can we go get help now?"

Maria slipped her arm through Mina's. The pair of them were unsteady on their feet as they stumbled out of the apartment towards the lift. "We have to go to the thirteenth floor. My partner should be there." Maria jabbed her finger on the number thirteen and hoped that Frankie was okay. They fell out of the elevator on the thirteenth to see Frankie, Father Anthony, the security guard, Veronica and Stanley all standing in a circle outside the room. Frankie let go of Veronica's hand and ran towards Maria.

"What the hell? You're bleeding."

She looked at the deep cut on his cheek that was trickling blood. "So are you. Rickie tried to kill me. He stabbed the killer, too, but he's not himself. We managed to knock him out but he's in her apartment." She left out the part about the woman in blue distracting him long enough for them to attack him and make their escape. "He needs help, Father, spiritual help, because there is something dark inside him that doesn't belong there."

Veronica looked at Frankie. "We need to bring him here, where it all began." She got out of the wheelchair and Stanley took her arm. "Take my chair, tie him to it and bring him down here. I have a plan."

Buzz grabbed hold of the chair. "I keep telling you I don't get paid enough for this shit." But he pushed it towards the elevator. Frankie and Isaac followed. "Father, you wait here and keep an eye on the girls. Do what you got to do, and we'll go get him." Father Anthony nodded. Isaac turned and threw a door key at him. He looked at Maria. "Wait until we tell you what went down in here. You'll never believe it."

She smiled. "Father, I've seen dead bodies, ghosts, I've dealt with demons and traveled back in time to fight a soul collector—trust me, I'll believe it."

He leaned over and hugged her. "You are one tough broad, Maria."

"And you have been spending too much time with Frankie."

He grinned at her.

Veronica and Mina stared at Maria in amazement. "You've done what?"

"Long story—stories. What are we doing, are we going in?"

Veronica nodded. "We have to. Whatever it is that's been using this hotel as its hunting grounds needs to be stopped, and it all started in here, in this room."

Stanley, who hadn't said a word yet, shook his head. "It all started the moment they began building this place. I went through the records, everything I had on it. Underneath this plot of land lies probably in excess of ten thousand bodies. They bought the land for peanuts and built over it, not bothering to move the bodies, and they probably didn't bless the ground either. Washington Square Park and most of the parks in the city were burial grounds that were landscaped over. I don't know how they got permission to build this hotel on top of it, but they did, and here we are now."

Maria thought about James Carter. What else could he have unleashed? It wasn't too far away from here. This place was the perfect breeding ground for evil. "Let's go inside and wait for the guys to bring Rickie here before SWAT turn up and trample over everything. If we don't deal with it now, then it will keep on doing this. I don't want to be responsible for any more deaths inside this hotel."

Father Anthony opened the door and flicked on the lights. She turned to Father Anthony.

"You guys did that?"

"It was Frankie and Buzz."

Stanley nodded his head. "Rickie is going to be pissed when he sees it."

"Rickie has other problems to deal with at the moment. That hole is the least of them."

The door was thrown open as Frankie barged in with a semi-conscious Rickie in Veronica's wheelchair. "He's coming round. Get me something to secure him with."

Maria looked around. There were no sheets on the beds and the curtains hung in tatters. Veronica slipped the scarf she was wearing from around her neck and tossed it to Frankie, who used it to tie Rickie's hands together. "We haven't got much time, the cops are all over the place."

Veronica looked at Anthony. "If I can draw it out, can you do something with it?"

"I'll do my best."

She hobbled across the room until she faced Rickie, then she slapped him hard across the cheek.

"Arnie, you son of a bitch. Come out of there and fight like a man."

Rickie's eyes rolled to the back of his head with the force of the blow. Then they came into focus and fixed their gaze onto Veronica.

"You useless piece of shit, Arnie. I thought we were having a good time, and you went and cut off my foot. Do you know how difficult it is to walk around with only one foot? No, you asshole, you have no idea."

"Cherry." The voice was rough; it sounded as if it had woken from a deep sleep.

"Look, I know you couldn't help yourself, but I thought we could have been more than a one-night stand, you know? I thought maybe I could have meant something to you."

"Cherry."

"Yes, it's me. I bet you thought I died. Well, surprise, surprise. I didn't, and you owe me big time, Arnie. I'm gonna need you to do me a favor to make up for it." She glanced at Father Anthony who nodded. "I need you to leave Rickie alone. Come out of his body. Christ, I don't know what I'm doing talking to a dead guy. Except, you didn't die that night, did you? Whatever dragged you into the wall, it's kept you alive all these years in spirit."

"I can't... it won't let me."

"Yes, you can. Come to me, don't let it hold on to you any longer. I don't know if you're going to the light, Arnie, because you're such an asshole, but you don't have to be trapped here any longer. Come to me, let whatever darkness is keeping you there stay."

Father Anthony held out his hands and began to recite the last rites again. Veronica continued.

"Come on, Arnie, it's time to let go."

Tears filled Rickie's eyes as a dark shadow began to emerge from his body. The room was silent. Frankie had hold of Maria's arm and Buzz had hold of Mina's. The shadow took on the form of a man, and Veronica smiled at him. "We had a good night until you went and spoiled it. You know, I thought you were the best goddamn trick I ever turned until you chopped off my foot. But I forgive you, Arnie, and I want you to move on to a better place than this."

The ghostly man smiled at Veronica, as a beam of light shone down from above. It was so bright it was blinding. Father Anthony kept on praying. "It's time for you to move into the light now, may God have mercy on your soul."

Arnie whispered, "Sorry." It was so faint they only just heard it, and then he stepped into the light and with a blinding flash, the room fell into darkness, and he was gone.

"Where the fuck did he come from? And what in the name of God happened to that wall? Am I hallucinating? Tell me I am."

All eyes turned to Rickie. Frankie bent down and looked at him. "You good?"

"Good? I feel like crap and this room resembles a war zone." He turned to Maria in horror. "What happened to you?"

She refrained from telling him that *he* had happened to her. This was one huge mess that would take forever to sort out. Rickie had stabbed a guy while not in control of himself. That guy in return had attacked Mina while not in control of himself, and murdered Travis and two teen girls. But what judge was going to believe any of that?

"I need a stiff drink, Rickie, and you're buying. You owe me and Mina big time."

"I do? Well, can you untie me first? Who tied me up and why? Actually, I don't want to know. Just get me out of this room. Buzz, when we leave this room and that piece of shit skeleton in the wall has been collected, I want it sealed off, brick up the door, and hang a picture of Jesus over it. I don't care what anyone says, but do not let anyone else in here after the cops have finished."

Buzz nodded. "Yes, sir."

Frankie untied his hands. "You better let Veronica have her chair back. She lost her foot a long time ago and has never found it. Lost property told her she didn't have a leg to stand on."

Veronica laughed. "Not bad, not bad, just don't give up the day job yet, Frankie."

He held out a hand to Rickie and pulled him up. "Seriously, are you good, man? You feel like yourself?"

"I feel like a bag of crap, Frankie, but I'm good."

Veronica swapped places with him. As they all filed out of the room, she turned back and whispered, "God bless you, Arnie, because somebody has to."

Then Isaac slammed the door shut, just as a SWAT team burst out of the stairwell into the hallway. The guy at the front held up a hand. "Frankie, Maria, you guys okay?"

They nodded and he gave them the thumbs up before shouting down his radio for everyone to stand down. Rickie looked terrified. "You weren't kidding about them?"

"Nope, they came through, but like I said, we usually manage our own mess without their assistance."

They piled into the bar. The few guests in there stared at them in morbid fascination. Stanley took charge. "Bourbon shots all round." Maria downed hers, managing not to choke, and felt soothed by the burning inside her throat. She watched as Frankie picked his up, turning the glass around in his fingers, before putting it down on the bar. He smiled at her. "I've decided to make a few changes."

"You have?"

He nodded. "I'm giving up the booze and I'm thinking of handing in my notice as soon as I get back to the station. I'm sorry, Maria, but I can't do this again. It's too much and I can't take the stress of seeing you get hurt like this."

She reached out for his hand. "Frankie Conroy, I'm proud

of you. Please do exactly that, because I can't work like this either. Although I'm gonna miss you like crazy, and I don't even know if I could do this job without you. But I want to see you strolling around Coney Island in a pair of board shorts, living your life with Betsy Conner." She winked at him, and he bent down and kissed a spot on her face that was blood free.

"Thank you. That means a lot—and I want you to get in the back of the ambulance, go get checked out and have your face cleaned up. You're scaring the guests. I'll sort Rickie out, get a handle on this disaster zone, then pass it on to Cooper to deal with."

"Sounds like a plan. Don't forget the body up in Mina's apartment. The fake maintenance guy was stabbed by Rickie in self-defense. I checked his pockets on the way out, saw his driver's license. His address was next door to Travis's place. I think somehow the darkness spread to him. Maybe it decided Travis wasn't strong enough to carry out the murders, who knows?"

"Whoever he is, I'll sort it. He saved your life, and it's corny, but you're all I have."

She smiled at him, then remembered what else they had to do. "And you'll call the girls' families? Tell them we've caught the killer? They don't have to know the rest just yet... only that justice is served. Then call Harrison for me, will you?"

The captain in charge of SWAT walked into the bar with Addison, who took one look at the unlikely group of survivors and shook his head. "What a shit show, Miller, Conroy. What the hell happened here? And Miller, why do you look as if you died last week?" He turned and waved a group of paramedics in, who were standing at the entrance. "If you refuse to go with them, Miller, you're fired, because you look like crap."

"I feel like it. I'm not arguing with you."

"Christ, you're concussed." He turned to Father Anthony. "Sorry, Father." Father Anthony held up a hand, then passed the glass to the bartender to fill up. Addison looked at them all, one by one.

"Miller, this case must have been bad if you've got the good father here taking shots of bourbon. I don't even know if I want to hear it. I've got acid in my chest just thinking about what you're going to tell me."

She closed her eyes. "I'm done, shout at me later."

Addison pointed to her. "Get her a chair and get her to the ER."

The medics did just that. And as they wheeled Maria out into the late evening sun, she inhaled deeply. She was glad to be alive—and even happier that she wouldn't have to come back here again.

TEN DAYS LATER

Emilia's funeral was a quiet, beautiful affair just like the woman herself had been in life. Maria had held onto Missy's hand the entire time, scared that if she let go, Maria would be the one to fall to the ground and wail. Her grief was so consuming that she didn't think she'd ever get over the loss of this beautiful woman, who'd come into her life far too late. As Father Anthony closed the service, the few mourners turned and walked away, leaving Maria and Missy staring down into the hole in the ground at the simple, white casket inside.

"I can't believe she's gone. I'm so sorry, Missy, this is all my fault."

Missy turned to her. "Look, Maria, no offence, but we were both old. It was going to happen at some point. Death is one thing none of us can avoid and you blaming yourself isn't going to bring her back. You didn't force us to come to the Parker. You never asked us to. Emilia said she needed to go, so I agreed, and we dragged poor Father Anthony along for the ride. Her heart gave out and she died. Her earthly body might not be here but because of you, we got to be together for two glorious years and that is more than I ever thought would be possible. Besides, she's said you have to stop moping around because it's depressing."

Maria cried into a Kleenex that Frankie had passed to her. "She said what?"

"She said woman up."

"How do you know that?"

"I'll tell you how I know. The damn broad came to her own funeral." Missy pointed to a beautiful oak tree in the distance. "She's been standing over there watching the entire time, putting me off." She raised her voice. "It's hard to concentrate, Em, when you are gawping at us all to see what we're doing and if we're crying enough."

Maria couldn't help but laugh, blotting her eyes with the tissue. "She's really over there? You're not saying that to make me feel better?"

"Honey, I wouldn't lie to you about something like that. She said hi. She loves you very much. And there is one last thing she needs from you."

"Tell her I love her, and I'll do anything."

"I don't think you love her this much." Missy glanced over at the tree. "I'm doing it, give me a chance. She's still bossing me around, the bare cheek of it. Anyhow, she wants you to take Father Anthony and go back to the Parker."

"Why?" Maria felt sick at the thought of going anywhere near that hotel.

"She said it's time we helped Isabelle Winter move on. She's spent far too long trapped in that place."

"The woman in blue?"

Missy nodded. "The woman in blue. Emilia will help guide her. She just needs you to go and find her because you can see her."

Maria didn't elaborate and tell Missy that every time she'd seen the woman in blue, she'd almost died.

"Em said that she'll take care of you. There is nothing to

fear from that place anymore. She is your guardian angel now and will protect you."

"We best go tell Father Anthony the good news then."

"He already knows and is ready to go—only because Em asked. He said he'd do it after the service, but that he wasn't going anywhere near that hotel ever again after."

Maria looked around the cemetery. The only car left was a black Lincoln limousine parked beside where Father Anthony stood chatting with the driver and Frankie. Missy linked her arm around Maria's, and they walked towards them.

The limousine stopped at the entrance to the Parker and the driver helped Missy out. Frankie held out a hand for Maria, who didn't argue with him. Father Anthony got out last. "I can't believe we're going back inside this place of our own free will."

Missy smiled. "I know, I'm sorry to drag you back, but Em was quite insistent."

None of them questioned her. They trusted Missy, and they loved her and Emilia deeply. If this was Emilia's last wish, who were they to not carry it out?

Maria didn't look up: she wanted to see Isabelle Winter on her terms.

Shanice, who was at the reception desk, took one look at them and waved a hand in the air to acknowledge their presence, then she looked back down at whatever was more interesting on her phone.

Missy pressed the call button for the tenth floor and Maria found it hard to breathe, as if she was purposefully going to find the ghost that had told her she was going to die not once, but twice. Frankie and Missy hung back, letting Maria and Father Anthony lead the way out of the elevator.

Maria stared at the window in the hallway but was unable to see any hint of blue whatsoever. "I don't think she's here."

Missy gently pushed her forward. "She's here. Go talk to her."

Maria walked towards the window. "Isabelle, are you here?" Nothing happened, but Maria kept on talking. "I did some research about what happened to you when I was stuck in the hospital, and I thought you'd like to know about your daughter." She paused as the air directly in front of her rippled slightly like it did on a hot summer's day and a blue dress began to come into view. "Faith was a brilliant woman, and she was devastated by your death, but she did great things in her life, all because of her love for you. She went on to set up a suicide helpline in the city and because of her, thousands of lives were saved. She loved you so much."

Tears pricked Maria's eyes, making her vision blurry. As she blinked them away, she saw Isabelle staring at her, waiting for her to continue. "It's time to leave this place, Isabelle. You've spent so long here. It's time to move on now. Faith is waiting for you. Don't you want to see her again?"

Isabelle's voice was soft and gentle. "I would love that more than anything in this world, but I can't leave this place. I'm stuck here for all eternity. I do my best to warn people they need to take care and that's all I can do."

"You can leave, I promise you can. Father Anthony will help you. He's the bravest, kindest priest I ever met, and he will guide you. Take my arm and we'll go out into the street, into the light, and out of the darkness."

Maria felt an icy hand on her arm and looked to see Isabelle standing next to her. The woman nodded once with a faint smile across her lips, as if she hoped it was true but dared not believe it, and they all stepped into the elevator. As the doors opened to the foyer, Isabelle let go of Maria's arm. Maria could sense the woman's hesitation and Maria reached out for her hand again. "We can do this. We are going to do this."

Isabelle nodded. "What if I can't go to the light?"

"You will go to the light, trust me."

Father Anthony smiled at them both. "Isabelle, I can't see you like my friend here but I'm here to tell you that you will be welcomed into the light with open arms. You have nothing to fear. You have spent far too long in this darkness and my friend here will help you if you're ready."

Isabelle looked longingly out at the front entrance. "I think I am so ready, thank you."

Maria kept hold of her hand and gently tugged her forward, smiling. "No, thank you. You saved my life. I'm sorry that I didn't realize you were trying to help and that nobody was there to save your life, but I have a very dear friend who recently passed, and she is here to help you."

They walked out into the warm sunshine and Isabelle laughed with delight. Then she faltered, staring at the sidewalk on the opposite side of the road. A woman was standing next to Emilia, a look of deep longing and so much love on her face that it made Maria want to cry. The woman called out, "Mom?"

Isabelle let go of Maria's hand and a joyous smile spread across her face. "Faith, oh Faith, I missed you so much. I'm so sorry." She rushed across the empty street into her daughter's arms.

Maria didn't realize she was sobbing until Frankie, who was standing next to her, passed her his handkerchief. She saw him lift a sleeve to blot his own eyes and whispered, "Can you see them?" He nodded. When Maria turned back, they were fading out of sight. But not before Isabelle waved at Maria. Maria waved back and then let out a loud, hitching sob as both women faded completely.

"Stop it, you're gonna make me ugly cry in the street."

She elbowed him but laughed at the same time. "These are happy tears; I feel so glad we got to help her."

"You helped her. You have a gift for this, Maria," said Father

Anthony next to her. "Maybe you could do this full time... you know, as a job."

Maria shook her head. "I never asked for any of this. I'm more at home chasing the bad guys who I can stick a pair of cuffs on and fight with if I have to. I think I'm going to see if I can go back to my old job. And if I can't, then I'm going to think about opening up a bookstore with my new business partner, Harrison. What about you, Frankie?"

He nodded. "I don't know what to do. Whatever it is, I don't want to work without you. I think I've had enough of this. Thirty years being a cop and the last three cases have been more than my old brain can cope with. I've been thinking about what you said, Maria. I need to start enjoying my life and I want you to as well. I don't want to be worrying about what you're doing every day. A bookstore sounds a lot safer than this." He pointed to the Parker.

She grinned at him. "Would a certain medical examiner have anything to do with this sudden change of heart?"

He shrugged. "Maybe, but I think it's time to slow things down."

She reached out and squeezed his hand. "I think you're absolutely doing the right thing, Frankie. I'll miss you, but I will be coming to visit if you move to Coney Island. Maybe you and Stanley could start a beach bar or something and we can all hang out together drinking martinis and watching the sun set? Harrison might be your business partner, too. He's got a heart of gold and it's in the right place. I think I fell on my feet when he decided not to give up on me."

"What have I been telling you, kid? He's a rich guy that isn't an asshole. There aren't many of those around. Chances like that don't come around often. And you know what... I like the idea of a beach bar. Or maybe I'll just hang around at Stanley's place. Whatever I do, I'd sure miss working with you, kid. But I wouldn't miss the monsters."

Frankie leaned over and ruffled Maria's hair. And for the first time she didn't admonish him. She let him have this moment, because she loved him. He was her best friend, and she was happy they both had bright futures ahead of them—futures she'd never have foreseen in a million years.

A LETTER FROM THE AUTHOR

Huge thanks for reading *The Girls on Floor 13*. I hope you were hooked on Maria and Frankie's third journey. If you want to join other readers in hearing all about my new releases and bonus content, you can sign up for my newsletter!

www.stormpublishing.co/helen-phifer

If you enjoyed this book and could spare a few moments to leave a review that would be hugely appreciated. Even a short review can make all the difference in encouraging a reader to discover my books for the first time. Thank you so much!

I've always wanted to write a scary story set in a haunted hotel; I think it was on my list of things to write before I even got published—ever since I read *The Shining* by Stephen King many moons ago. That book stayed with me and in the many hotels I've stayed in since, I always hope that I won't see the Grady twins or find Redrum written on the door in red crayon.

Then I went to New York and as I was walking around, the characters for Maria and Frankie popped into my head and I knew that one day I would pitch them both against a crazed killer in a haunted hotel. It just had to be done and it was quite a challenge, but a hugely enjoyable one for me as a writer. The words flow so much better when you're having fun whilst writing a story.

I got a lot of inspiration from this book from the famous Chelsea Hotel—the true-life stories of what has happened in there are beyond anything I could make up. I liked the iconic style of the Chelsea's exterior, which is why you may recognize the description of the Parker is similar. Stanley was the manager of the Chelsea Hotel, although my Stanley is more of a Phifer-style creation. I also was influenced by the scariest film I watched as a teenager, *A Nightmare on Elm Street*, when I created the demon haunting people in their dreams.

I'm sad that Missy and Emilia's beautiful relationship has come to an end in their mortal lives, but long may it continue. Proof that I like to believe our souls live on when we die and that some people will always be with you, no matter what, because we keep them alive in our hearts until the day we meet again.

Thanks again for being part of this amazing journey with me and I hope you'll stay in touch—I have so many more stories and ideas to entertain you with!

Love
Helen xx

facebook.com/Helenphifer1
x.com/helenphifer1
instagram.com/helenphifer
tiktok.com/@helen.phifer

ACKNOWLEDGMENTS

As always, a huge thank you to my lovely editor Kate Smith for making this so much better than the version I sent her. I always say it takes a whole team to make the book you are reading sparkle, and she certainly does.

Another thank you to the fabulous Natasha Hodgson for her hard work in copyediting this story. Thank you to the lovely Alexandra Holmes and the rest of the amazing Storm team for every part you have played in making this story what it is.

Thank you to Amanda Rutter for her proofreading skills.

Thank you as always to the brilliant Oliver Rhodes for letting me bring these stories to life.

A huge shout out to the amazing Stephanie Cannon for her audiobook narration, it's just superb and I know my readers love listening to you so much. Also, the rest of the audiobook team, thank you for all your hard work.

A heartfelt thank you to my amazing proofreader extraordinaire Paul O'Neill who is so supportive and the biggest life saver there is.

The biggest thank you goes to you, my wonderful reader. I can't ever thank you enough for picking my book out of the many out there and reading it. Your support is what makes me able to do this fabulous job day in day out, getting these ideas out of my head and onto the page for you to read. You have no idea how much I appreciate every single one of you. You make my heart sing and I'm eternally grateful to you.

Thank you to my book club, those guys are there for the

book recommendations we like and don't like, except for Krog who is temporarily banned from choosing because, well, he knows why 😊 What happens in book club stays in book club. They have broadened my reading so much over the last four years and although we don't always talk about books as much as we should, we do have a laugh and they are very gracious when I force one of mine on them.

Thank you to my coffee gals Sam Thomas and Tina Sykes; where I would be without your weekly meetings to keep me sane, I don't know. I love you both lots.

Lastly a huge thank you to my family, for all the love and entertainment. Sometimes it's like an episode of *Shameless*, but no matter what, I love you all and I'm so proud of every one of you.

Until next time, take care and much love to you all.

Helen xx

Printed in Great Britain
by Amazon

42513830R00142